The Usual Suspects
Staff

Editor R. V. Branham

Co-editor M.F. McAuliffe

Office Mgr. Sofia Sensei Satori Šostakovna Satyagraha Stoličniya Sashimi Shitkicker

Assoc. Editor T. Warburton y Bajo

Contrib. Editors T. Warburton y Bajo & Channing Dodson & Michael Lohr & Douglas Spangle

Field Correspondent Michael Lohr

House Tr. T. Warburton y Bajo (Sp.), Miguel Caminhão (Portuguese), チャニング・ドッドソン (Japanese). Алекса Сигала & Андрей Сен-Сеньков (Russian), Ani Gjika (Albanian), Anggo Genorga (Tagalog), Michael Lohr (Scand.) & rvb (Sp., & select Eng.), & Ana Katana & Dijana Jacovak (Croatian) & a cohort of Lithuanian translators

House Spanish Copyediting Lyda Alvarez, M.F. McAuliffe

Cover Illo Graham K. Willoughby *Design* T. Warburton y Bajo

Cover comix & phfoto illos & franking var. Postal Services

Photos (except as noted) M. F. McAuliffe, T. Warburton y Bajo

Layout T. Warburton y Bajo & R. V. Branham

Prod. Tools InDesign, Photoshop (occasionally, when functional), Gimp, Dreamscope

Tech Support Sam Ward

Additional Editorial & Design Assistance Douglas Spangle & M.F. McAuliffe

Legal Peter Shaver/Sound Advice LLC

Publisher GobQ LLC/Reprobate Books

Double Trouble Flipbook double Issues printed Nov. & May of ea. year.

Post-production printing Ingram Spark/Lightning Source

Also distrib. & printed nationally & internationally through Ingram Spark/Lightning Source POD

Sold through independent bookstores & available through Ingram & amazon dot com & GobshiteQuarterly dot com

P.R. P. H. Vazak

Gobshite Quarterly: Double Trouble, Nos. 35/36, Winter & Spring 2020

$12.00 US

ISBN 978-1-68454-470-7

GobQ volunteers: Qualified candidates please send résumé to

GobQ LLC, 338 NE Roth St., Portland, OR 97211, or to gobq at yahoo dot com

Gobshite Quarterly

Double Trouble / Issue 35 – Winter 2020

This issue is dedicated to the memory of:

Les Murray (17 Oct., 1938 — 29 Apr., 2019)
Sylvia Miles (9 Sept., 1924 — 12 June, 2019)
Kevin Killian (24 Dec., 1952 — 15 June, 2019)
[Lady] Brenda Maddox [FRSL] (24 Feb., 1932 — 16 June, 2019)
Irene Coates (née Gregory) (23 Mar., 1925 — 18 June 2019
Geraldine Millais Harcourt (25 May, 1952 — 21 June, 2019)
Édith Scob (21 Oct., 1937 — 26 June 2019)
Ennio Guarnieri (12 Oct., 1930 — 1 July, 2019)
Freddie Jones (12 Sept., 1927 — 9 July, 2019)
Rip Torn (6 Feb., 1931 — 9 July, 2019)
Isaac Lesiba Maphotho (26 Feb., 1931 — 13 July, 2019)
Naomi Ishida 石田 奈央美 (6 Aug., 1969 — 18 July, 2019)
Yoshiji Kigami 木上 益治 (28 Dec., 1957 — 18 July, 2019)
Futoshi Nishiya 西屋 太志 (1981 — 18 July, 2019)
Yasuhiro Takemoto (武本 康弘 (5 Apr., 1972 — 18 July, 2019)
Rutger Hauer (23 Jan., 1944 — 19 July, 2019)

Art Neville (17 Dec., 1937 — 22 July, 2019)
Hal Prince (30 Jan., 1928 — 31 July, 2019)
D.A. Pennebaker (15 July, 1925 — 1 Aug., 2019)
Toni Morrison (18 Feb., 1931 — 5 Aug., 2019)
Larry Siegel (29 Oct., 1925 — 20 Aug., 2019)
Elaine Feinstein (24 Oct., 1930 – 23 Sept., 2019)
Jacques Chirac (29 Nov., 1932 — 26 Sept., 2019)
Gennadi Manakov Геннадий Манаков (1 June, 1950 — 26 Sept., 2019)
Joseph Charles Wilson (6 Nov., 1949 — 27 Sept., 2019)
José José (17 Feb., 1948 — 28 Sept., 2019)
Jessye Norman (15 Sept., 1945 — 30 Sept., 2019)
Ginger Baker (19 Aug., 1939 — 6 Oct., 2019)
Giya Kancheli (გია ყანჩელი) (10 Aug., 1935 — 2 Oct., 2019)
Ciaran Carson (9 Oct., 1948 — 6 Oct., 2019)
Robert Forster (13 July, 1941 — 11 Oct., 2019)

12.00 USDOL || € 8.03462 EURO || £ 6.36 GBP (UK) || $ 12.0281 AUD (Oz) || $11.4795 CAN || ¥ 1,179.53 JPY (japan yen) || 115.380 SAR (S. Africa)

12.00 USDOL || € 8.03462 EURO || £ 6.36 GBP (UK) || $ 12.0281 AUD (Oz) || $11.4795 CAN || ¥ 1,179.53 JPY (japan yen) || 115.380 SAR (S. Africa)

Gobshite Quarterly
Double Trouble / Issue 36 – Spring 2020

Nastashia Minto, in front of one of Menkaure's subsidary pyramids, & in front of the Sphinx, in the Giza necropolis, outside Giza City, Egypt, Sept., 2019.

Respectfully flip the book over, as Issue 36, Spring 2020, is a whole upsy-daisy 68 pgs away fr. the Winter 2020 issue

Gob Words A word to give offense, when offense may be due. ***Gobshite***, per OED, is what the American crew of Adm. Perry's Expedition to Japan were called by the natives; Amer. Heritage Dictionary, 4th. ed., refers to a wad of expectorated chaw & to the Old Eng. *Shiten*; yet another dictionary refers to a Gobshite as a "*pernicious blatherskite*"— i.e., a stiff to read the teleprompter feed for CNN or Rupert Murdoch's Fox "*News*" bullshit mtn. & those offended by the word can now be offended trilingually & quadrilingually, because all English-lang. pces have a foreign lang. *en-face* escort, whether Spanish, Croatian, Slovenian, Macedonian, Greek, Arabic, Icelandic, Farsi, Albanian, Finnish, Danish, French, Portuguese, Italian, Russian, Lithuanian, Gaelic, Japanese, Korean, Tagalog, or whatever language puts on it UN Observer cap. Wasn't it Pulitzer who said that journalism should comfort the afflicted & afflict the comfortable? Finally, a Rosetta Stone for the New World Order.

Meanwhile, in the irreal world, early *GobQ* contributors Les Murray & Kevin Killian passed away earlier this year. On a more felicitous not we have a congressional impeachment train. & to balance that out, on the other side of the pond there's this Brexit thing that persists in mutating & morphing & driving Brits batfuck. Oh, & millions of disaffected people taking to the streets in Barcelona, Beirut, Hong Kong, London, Paris, Santiago, & other cities; there are sit-ins in museums, again over criminal activities of many generous museum board members & donors; middle aged white dudes are terrified of a young Danish teeny-bopper who is calling everyone out on climate change. & Isis has a new caliph. As Bertie Brecht said, *pity not the nation that lacks super heroes, pity the nation that* wants *superheroes.*

The Usual Suspects
Contributors

Miglė Anušauskaitė, who studied semiotics at Vilniaus U., who works at Judaikos tyrimų centras, pt. of Lietuvos nacionalinė Martyno Mažvydo biblioteka, & whose comix lurk on *ihavenoteeth.com*, returns w/a viscerally ecstatic *summer feels/vasaros jausmai/sumar finnst/ljetno doba/verano siente* (Eng./Lith/Icel./Croat/Sp.); keep watching the skies.

Veronica Dintinjana, whose 1st. coll. of pomes, *Rumeri Gromi Grm Forzicij/Yellow Burns for the Forsythia Bush* won the Best 1st. Book Award, is resident doctor at a local hospital. She returns w/Slovenian tr. of Oz poet Les Murray, done in collab. w/her sister *Mia Dintinjana*: D.C., *At University/Na Univerzi, Experience/Izkušnja, Portrait of a Felspar-coloured Cat/Portret mačke v barvi peska v glini, Fusée/Sprožilni mehanizem, The Young Fox/Lisjaček, Pietà, Once Attributed to Cosme Tura/Pietà, nekoč pripisana Cosimu Turi* (pome)(pessem).

Boris Gregorić returns to *GobQ* w/an Eng. tr. of Croatian poet Miroslav Kirin's *About the Pencil/O olovci* (pome)(pjesma).

Dijana Jakovac returns w/ Croatian tr. of Swiss poet Clemens Umbricht's pome, *Die Rückkehr des Odysseus/The Return of Odysseus/Povratak Odiseja.* (Gedicht)(pome)(pjesma).

Ana Katana returns to *GobQ* w/ her Croat. tr. of Oz poet Les Murray's *D.C., At University/Na Fakultetu, Experience/Izkustvo, The Young Fox/Mlada Lisica, Pietà, Once Attributed to Cosme Tura/Pietà, nekoć pripisivana Cosimu Turi* (pome)(pjesma), of Croatian comix artist Helena Klačocar-Vusksić's *Elle est trop petite.../She's too small...,Premalena je...* (portfolio), & Little Beirut author Matthew Robinson's story *Boomtown Love/Kad žila presahne* (story)(priča).

Christoph Keller, now ensconced in St. Galen, Switz., offers his memories of Les Murray.

Miroslav Kirin, living in Zagreb, returns w/several recent pomes, *O olovci/About the Pencil, Jalog br. 39/ iLogue no 39, Jalog br. 41/iLogue no 41, Jalog br. 42/ iLogue no 42, Jalog br. 60/iLogue no 60* (pjesma)(pome).

Helena Klačocar-Vusić, raised in Bosnia, was co-founder of the Zagreb artistic grp. ZZOT, published an award-winning graphic novel based on her yr. at sea, & thru her involvement w/ Wild Eye Grp. made her name at festivals & exhibitions in recent yrs. This pce is excerpted fr. a comic orig. published in Fr., hence the title: *Elle est trop petite.../She's too small...,Premalena je...* (portfolio).

Martina Kramer did the French tr. of Croatian writer Miroslav Kirin's pomes, *O olovci/About the Pencil/ À propos du crayon, & Jalog br. 60/ Nulogue, n° 60/iLogue no. 60* (pjesma)(poeme)(pome).

Пвел Лемберский/Pavel Lembersky returns w/ a Russian tr. of Oz poet Les Murray's *The Young Fox/Лисенок* (pome)(стихотворéние).

Michael Lohr returns w/Icel. tr. of Oz poet Les Murray's *DC, At University/Í Háskóla, Portrait of a Felspar-coloured Cat/Mynd af Felspar-litarði kött* (pome)(ljóð), Little Beirut author Matthew Robinson's story *Boomtown Love/Boomtown ást* (story)(saga), & icelandic txto for Miglė Anušauskaitė's comic *summer feels/vasaros jausmai/sumar finnst* (comix)(komiksas)(teiknimyndasaga).

Vanda Mikšić did the French tr. of Croatian poet Miroslav Kirin's *Jalog br. 41/ Nulogue, n° 41/iLogue no 41, & Jalog br. 42/ Nulogue, n° 42/iLogue no 42*

(pjesma)(poeme)(pome).

Les Murray, among our very first contribs., sadly, returns for his last call. We offer several pomes, in several languages. The Eng. titles: *D.C., At University, Experience, Portrait of a Felspar-coloured Cat, Fusée, The Young Fox, Pietà, Once Attributed to Cosme Tura.* A resident of Bunyah, in NSW, his books of pomes incl. *The Weatherboard Cathedral, The Venacular Republic, Ethnic Radio, Subhuman Redneck Poems* (T.S. Eliot Prize), & his books of essays incl. *The Peasant Mandarin, The Quality of Spread, & Killing the Black Dog.*

Dominykas Norkūnas returns w Lith. tr. of Oz poet Les Murray's *D.C./Vašintonas* (pome)(poema).

Jelena Pataki returns w. Croatian tr. of Oz poet Les Murray's *Portrait of a Felspar-coloured Cat/Portret mačke boje feldspata & Fusée/Fitilj,* Rimas Uzgiris' *Human Conditional: a Triptych/Ljudski kondicional: Triptih* (pome)(pjesma), & Miglė Anušauskaitė's *summer feels/ljetno doba* (comic)(comíc).

Brankica Radić did the French tr. of Croatian poet Miroslav Kirin's *Jalog br. 42/ Nulogue, n° 42/iLogue no. 42* (pjesma)(poeme)(pome).

Matthew Robinson returns w/short story *Boomtown Love,* also incl. in the anthol. *The Jesus He Deserved & Other Thoughts on War & on Returning,* fr. GobQ/ Reprobate Books, avail. online at gobshitequarterly.com, or fr. yr bookstore.

Андрей Сен Сеньков returns w/ a Russ. tr. of Oz poet Les Murray's *At University/В Университете* (pome)(стихотворéние).

Douglas Spangle, Holbrook Award-winning Little Beirut poet & tr. returns w/ Eng. tr. of Clemens Umbricht's *Die Rückkehr des Odysseus/The Return of Odysseus* (das Gedicht)(pome).

Džiugas Stanevičius did the Lith. tr. for Croatian poet Miroslav Kirin's *Jalog br. 60/iLogue no 60/ manoLogas nr. 60* (pjesma)(pome)(poema).

Clemens Umbricht, Swiss poet, returns w/*Die Rückkehr des Odysseus/The Return of Odysseus* (Gedicht)(pome).

Rimas Uzgiris, Vilnius poet & prof., returns w/*Human Conditional: a Triptych/Žmogaus būklinis: Triptikas* (pome)(poema).

T. Warburton y Bajo y rvb did co-tr. of a baker's doz. of this issue's works into Spanish.

Graham Willoughby, whose artwork's adorned our covers since is. no. 2, returns, & still in watery colour! Graham has exhibited in galleries in the US, Germany & his native Oz, & has artist books in museum colls. worldwide.

9/11, the 1st. anno of the Al Qaida World Trade Ctr performative pce., & the 29th. anno of the CIA-engineered Pinochet coup in Santiago, Chile. *What else to do but see the artpunk band, Wire?—the longest running band this side of the Rolling Stones.* The Crystal Ballroom, with its orig. springy dance floor, is an often dodgy space, accoustically, & Wire is an odd band, in its demographic appeal. The age range of those attending was 14 to 75. Most of the teenagers were *not* in attendance with their parents. They were cordoned off from the beer garden. Most adults sat up in the bleachers, with beer or wine. When the music began, my water bottle shook; earplugs prevented my cranium rattling. — *rvb*

D. C.

City where aircraft are hung
as art, and security admits people
to the colonnaded floors
of horizontal beige skyscrapers
haunted by ideals and vast men.

— *Les Murray*

D. C.

Borg þar sem loftfar er hengt
sem list og öryggi viðurkennir fólk
til colonnaded gólf
lárétt beige skýjakljúfa
reimt af hugsjónarmönnum og miklum
mönnum.

— *Les Murray*
(Þýtt úr Ensku, Michael Lohr)

D. C.

Mesto, kjer letala obešajo
kot umetnost in varnostniki spuščajo ljudi
v nadstropja s kolonadami
vodoravnih bež nebotičnikov,
kjer strašijo ideali in široki možje.

— *Les Murray*
(Prevedli Mia in Veronika Dintinjana)

D.C.

Grad u kojem letjelice vješaju
kao umjetnine, i osiguranje propušta ljude
u kolonadne katove
vodoravnih bež nebodera
koje progone duhovi ideala i golemih ljudi.

— Les Murray
(Prijevod, Ana Katana)

Vašintonas

Miestas, kuriame orlaiviai iškabinami
lyg meno kūriniai, apsauginiai
praleidžia
žmones į gulstų dangoraižių rusvas
kolonadas, kur vaidenas idealai
ir didvyriai.

— Les Murray
(Vertė Dominykas Norkūnas)

D. C.

Ciudad en donde los aviones cuelgan
como arte, y la seguridad admite a la
gente
en los pisos columnatos
de rascacielos horizontales color beis
embrujados por ideales y hombres
vastos.

— Les Murray
(traducción, T. Warburton y Bajo y rob)

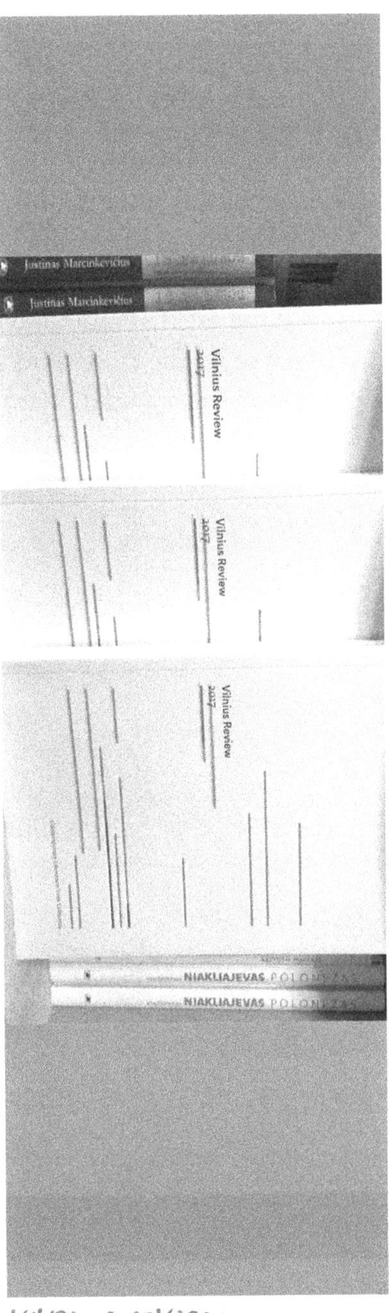

Vilnius review
Sirvydo St. 6,
LT — 01101
Vilnius, Lithuania
VilniusReview.com

AT UNIVERSITY

Puritans reckoned the cadavers
in Anatomy were drunks off the street;
idealists said they were benefactors
who had willed their bodies to science,
but the averted manila-coloured
people on the tables had pinned-back
graves excavated in them
around which they lay scattered in the end
as if exhumed from themselves.

— Les Murray

Í HÁSKÓLA

Puritans taldi lík
í líffærafræði voru drukkinn af götunni;
idealists sögðu að þeir væru velþegnar
sem hafði viljað líkama sínum að vísindum,
en afviða Manila-litað
fólk á borðum hafði fest aftur
grafir grafinn í þeim
þar sem þeir voru dreifðir í lokin
eins og ef þeir eru búnir að hrifsa sig.

— Les Murray
(Þýtt úr Ensku, Michael Lohr)

New So. Wales, Oz

NA UNIVERZI

Puritanci so menili, da so trupla
za ure anatomije pijanci, pobrani s ceste;
idealisti so rekli, da so to dobrotniki,
ki so svoje telo zapustili znanosti,
toda zaobiti ljudje v barvi rjavega ovojnega papirja
na mizah so imeli razprte
grobove izkopane v njih samih,
okoli njih so na koncu raztrošeni ležali,
kakor bi jih iz njih samih izkopali.

— *Les Murray*
(Prevedli Mia in Veronika Dintinjana)

NA FAKULTETU

Puritanci su leševe s anatomije
smatrali pijancima s ulice;
idealisti su ih nazivali dobročiniteljima
koji su tijela posvetili znanosti,
ali žućkasti ljudi
izvraćeni na stolovima
umjesto trbuha imahu
pribadačama pričvršćene grobove
oko kojih su na kraju ležali rasuti
kao ekshumirani sami iz sebe.

— *Les Murray*
(Prijevod, Ana Katana)

В УНИВЕРСИТЕТЕ

Пуритане считали, что трупами
в анатомическом театре были пьяницы с улицы;
идеалисты говорили, что это жертвователи,
завещавшие свои тела науке,
но отвратильного манильского цвета
люди прижались друг к другу на столах,
раскопанные в них могилы
вокруг которых они теперь лежали,
были позже опустошены,
словно эксгумировали сами себя.

— Лес Муррай
(перевóд, Андрей Сен-Сеньков)

En la universidad

Los puritanos calcularon que los cadáveres
en Anatomía eran borrachos de la calle;
los idealistas dijeron que eran benefactores
que habían legado sus cuerpos a la ciencia,
pero las personas de color manila
en las mesas tenían
tumbas excavadas en ellas
alrededor de las cuales yacían dispersadas al final
como si se huberan exhumado ellas mismas.

— *Les Murray*
(traducción, T. Warburton y Bajo y rvb)

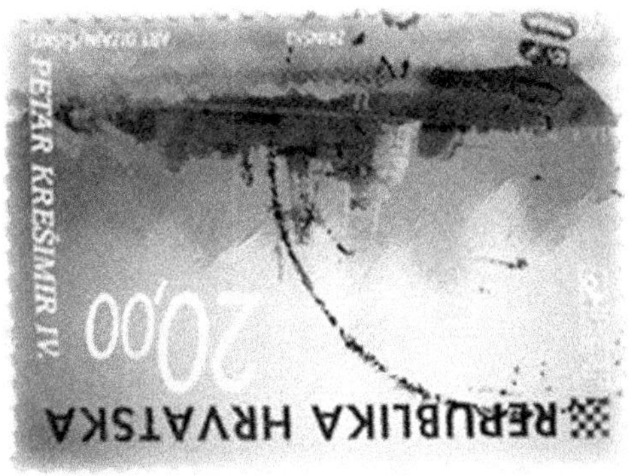

IZKUŠNJA

Slišal sem mačko zajavkati kakor lisico,
javsk! Ker je močnejše predenje avtomobila
ni pomirilo, zaprto v zaboj za mačke,
in je štopar rekel, *Imam kačo,*
da bo polovila podgane! Za božjo voljo.
Slišal sem kačo sikati po človeško.
videl sem gos jadrati kot drevesno skorjo,
slišal sem moža drkati gosaka —

— *Les Murray*
(Prevedli Mia in Veronika Dintinjana)

New So. Wales, Oz

EXPERIENCE

I heard a cat bark like a fox
Yah! because the car's larger purr
didn't soothe her, locked in a cat-box
and the hitchhiker *said I've got a snake*
to eat my rats! For Heavens sake.
I've heard a snake hiss like a man
I saw a goose sail like a bark
I heard a man wank like a goose —

— *Les Murray*

ISKUSTVO

Čuo sam mačku da laje k'o lija
Jah! motor može glasnije presti
Al' nikakve koristi, kad je moram zaključati.
Stoper reče *Meni štakore*
lovi zmija! Isuse, ova vožnja mi ne prija.
Čuo sam zmiju da sikće poput čovjeka
i gusku sam vidio da jedri glatko k'o brod
i čak muškarca kako ga gladi k'o guska.

— *Les Murray*
(Prijevod, Ana Katana)

Experiencia

Oí a un gato ladrar como una zorra
Yah! por que el ronroneo más grande del coche
no lo calma, encerrado en una caja para gatos
y el viajero de autopista dijo *¡tengo una serpiente*
para comer mis ratas! Por el amor de Dios.
He oído una serpiente silbar como un hombre
vi un ganso darse a la vela como una barca
oí a un hombre hacerse una paja como un ganso —

— *Les Murray*
(traducción, T. Warburton y Bajo y rob)

MYND AF FELSPAR-LITAÐRI KÖTT

Kærandi, hún nefndi sig Min
í overhanging heiminum.

Áferð hennar stjórnar sjálfum sér;
halastjarna hennar er Abyssinian.

Öll upplýsingaöflun hennar
er glæsileika.

Aldrei myndi jarðvegur hún flicked upp
viðvarandi í magafeldi hennar.

— *Les Murray*
(Þýtt úr Ensku, Michael Lohr)

Portrait of a Felspar-Coloured Cat

Plaintive, she named herself Min
in the overhanging world.

Her texture manages itself;
her comet tail is Abyssinian.

All her intelligence
is elegance.

Never would soil she flicked up
persist in her belly fur.

— *Les Murray*

Portret mačke boje feldspata

Potištena, nazvala se Min
u golemome svijetu.

Njezina tekstura vlada sobom;
njezin rep kao komet abesinski
je.

Sva je njezina inteligencija
elegancija.

Nikada joj prljavština koju zabaci
ne bi trajala u krznu trbuha.

— *Les Murray*
(prijevod, Jelena Pataki)

PORTRET MAČKE V BARVI PESKA V GLINI

Tožeča, poimenovala se je Min
v čez visečem svetu.

Njen vzorec skrbi sam zase;
rep, podoben kometu, je abesinski.

Vsa njena ostroumnost
je eleganca.

Prst, ki jo vrže v zrak,
se nikoli ne prime dlake na njenem trebuhu.

— *Les Murray*
(Prevedli Mia in Veronika Dintinjana)

Retrato de un gato de color felspar

Lamentosa, se nombró a sí misma Mín
en el mundo colgante.

Su textura se maneja a sí misma;
su cola de cometa es abisinia.

Toda su inteligencia
es elegancia.

Nunca persistía la tierra que escarbó
En el pelaje su vientre.

— *Les Murray*
(traducción, T. Warburton y Bajo y rob)

FUSÉE

A complex iron finial-head
still jazzling from the forge
smokes in its ash and sparkles
in the shadowy workshop —
but no:
    in fact it's a feathered
intricate protea bloom
haloed in a dusty ray of sun,
which in turn evades the stark
truth
    that it's an incandescent
missile tamped in the choke
of an 18th century mortar, aimed
to ignite a timber city.

— *Les Murray*

FITILJ

Složeni željezni vršak.
još blistav od kovanja
dimi se u svom pepelu i sjaji
u sjenovitoj radionici —
ali ne:
to je ustvari pernata
raskošna protea u cvatu
s aureolom od prašne zrake
        sunca
koja zauzvrat izbjegava oštru
istinu
da je to usijani
projektil nabijen u prigušivač
osamnaestostoljetnog
        minobacača,
s ciljem da zapali drveni grad.

— *Les Murray*
(prijevod, Jelena Pataki)

SPROŽILNI MEHANIZEM

Zapleten okrasni zaključek iz železa
še se blešči v dimu kovačije
iz pepela in iskri
v mračni delavnici –
toda ne:
    v resnici je peresno
fina protejska cvetlica,
ki jo obkroža prašen sončni sij,
a se zaradi njega izmika goli
resnici
        da je razžarjen
izstrelek, navit v primež
minometa iz 18. stoletja, namerjen
vžgati leseno mesto.

— *Les Murray*
(Prevedli Mia in Veronika Dintinjana)

Fusee

Una compleja cabeza de finial de hierro
todavía jazzervescente de la forja
fuma en sus cenizas y brilla
en el taller sombrío,
pero no:
    de hecho es una floración de protéa
intrincado con plumas
halado en un rayo polvoriento de sol,
que por su parte evade la verdad
se vera
        que es un incandescente
misil apisonado en el estrangulador
de un mortero del siglo xviii, dirigido
para encender una ciudad de madera.

— *Les Murray*
(traducción, T. Warburton y Bajo y rvb)

THE YOUNG FOX

I drove up to a young fox
on the disused highway.
It didn't scare, but watched me
roll up to it along the asphalt.
I got out. Any fowls it might kill
wouldn't be mine. No feud between us.

It watched quizzically, then bounded
away with an unmistakable headshake
that says *Play with me!*
and stopped, waiting. I remember
how deeply perfumed the leaves were
that lay on the pavement in that world.

— *Les Murray*

LISJAČEK

Ustavil sem se ob lisjačku
na zapuščeni cesti.
Ni se prestrašil, opazoval me je,
kako sem se privalil do njega po asfaltu.
Izstopil sem. Kokoši, ki jih bo morda
ugonobil, ne bodo moje. Med nama ni spora.

Opazoval je radovedno, nato je poskočil,
z nezmotljivim obračanjem glave,
ki pomeni: *Igraj se z mano!*
Se ustavil, čakal. Spominjam se,
kako močno je dišalo listje
na pločniku tistega sveta.

— *Les Murray*
(Prevedli Mia in Veronika Dintinjana)

New So. Wales, Oz

El zorro joven

Conduciendo me acerqué a un zorro joven
en una carretera desusada.
No se asustó, pero me miró
arrimarmele a lo largo del asfalto.
Me bajé. Cualquier ave que pudiese matar
no sería mía. Ninguna disputa entre nosotros.

Me miró con curiosidad, y luego se alejó
con un inequívoco movimiento de cabeza
que dice *¡juega conmigo!*
y se detuvo, esperando. Recuerdo
qué profundamente perfumadas eran las hojas
que yacían en el pavimento de aquel mundo.

— *Les Murray*
(traducción, T. Warburton y Bajo y rob)

MLADA LISICA

Dovezoh se do mlade lisice
na napuštenoj cesti.
Nije se prepala, nego me gledala
kako pristajem uz asfalt.
Izišao sam. Perad koju bi mogla
uloviti
neće pripasti meni. Nema zle krvi
među nama.

Ispitivački me posmatrala, zatim
krenula
naprijed kimajući kao
da veli *Igrajmo se!*
zastala je, pričekala me. Sjećam se
kako je opojno mirisalo lišće
ostavljeno na tlu toga svijeta.

— Les Murray
(Prijevod, Ana Katana)

Лисенок

К лисенку я подъехал
на заброшенном шоссе.
Не струсил он, но наблюдал,
как подкатил к нему я по асфальту.
Я вышел из машины. Дичь, что мог
убить он,
мне не досталась бы. И между нами не
было вражды.

Он с удивлением смотрел, затем
отпрянул,
подрагивая головой, что без сомненья
означало:
«Поиграй со мной!»
и в ожидании замер. Я припоминаю
глубокий аромат листвы,
что покрывала мостовую в том краю.

— Лес Маррей
(перевóд, Павел Лемберскӣ)

LAPUTĖ

Riedėdamas nenaudojamu plentu
aptikau mažą laputę.
Ji nepabūgo, tik stebėjo, kaip
aš privažiuoju arčiau jos.
Išlipau. Mano vištų ji nebūtų
pjovusi. Tarp mudviejų – jokios
nesantaikos.

Ji pašaipiai spoksojo į mane, tuomet
stryktelėjo į šoną ir papurtė snukutį,
kas be jokios abejonės reiškė *Eime
pažaist!*
Po to ji sustingo laukdama. Pamenu,
kaip sodriai kvepėjo medžių lapai,
nukloję šaligatvius tame pasaulyje.

— Les Murray
(Vertė Dominykas Norkūnas)

Pietà Once Attributed To Cosme Tura

This is the nadir of the story.

His mother's hairpiece her *sheitel,*
is torn away, her own cropped hair
looks burnt.
She had said the first Mass
and made Godhead a fact
which his strangeness had kept
proving,
but what of that is still true
now, with his limp weight at her
knee?
Her arms open, and withdraw,
and come back. That first eucharist
she could have been stoned to
death for
is still alive in her body.

— *Les Murray*

Pietà, nekoč pripisana Cosimu Turi

To je najnižja točka zgodbe.

Materino lasuljo, njen *šajtel,*
strgajo z glave, njeni kratki lasje so
videti ožgani.
Darovala je prvo mašo
in potrdila njegovo božjo naravo,
ki jo njegova čudnost kar naprej
potrjevala,
toda kaj od tega še drži,
zdaj, ko nosi njegovo mrtvo težo
na kolenih?
Njene roke se razprejo, se
umaknejo
in znova odprejo. Prvo obhajilo,
zaradi katerega bi jo lahko
kamenjali,
še živi v njenem telesu.

— *Les Murray*
(Prevedli Mia in Veronika Dintinjana)

New So. Wales, Oz

Pietà nekoć pripisivana Cosimu Turi

Ovdje priča ponire.

Majčino pokrivalo za glavu njezin
šejtel
otrgnut je, a ostrižena joj kosa
izgleda spaljeno.
Izgovorila je prvu Misu i
Božanstvo učinila činjenicom
koju je njegova čudnovatost iznova
potvrđivala,
ali što od toga ostaje istina
sada, kad on omlitavjelo leži na
njezinom koljenu?
Ruke joj se otvaraju, povlače u sebe,
i
vraćaju. Ta prva euharistija
koju je skoro platila kamenovanjem
još uvijek živi u njezinom tijelu.

— *Les Murray*
(Prijevod, Ana Katana)

Pietà una vez atribuido a Cosme Tura

Este es el nadir de la historia.

El postizo de su madre, su sheitel,
está despedazada, su propio pelo re-
cortado parece quemado.
Había dicho la primera Misa
e hizo al Altísimo una realidad
la que su extrañeza seguía demost-
rando,
¿pero qué de eso sigue cierto
ahora, con su peso flojo en su rodilla?
Sus brazos se abren, y se retiran,
y regresan. Esa primera eucaristía
por la que ella podría haber sido ape-
dreada hasta la muerte
sigue viva dentro de su cuerpo.

— *Les Murray*
(traducción, T. Warburton y Bajo y rvb)

Portfolio /
Elle est trop petite...,
Helena Klačocar-Vusksić

Premalena je...,
prijevod, Ana Katana

Ellla es demasiado pequeña, *traducción,*
T. Warburton y Bajo y rvb

Premalena je… bolje [bi bilo] da se ne miješa s ostalima.

Tako to počinje… „oni" i „mi"

She's too small ... [it'd be] better not to mingle with everyone.

that's how it starts ... with "them" and "us"

ELLA ES DEMASIADO PEQUEÑA ...[SERÍA] MEJOR NO MEZCLARSE CON LOS DEMÁS.

ASÍ ES COMO COMIENZAN LAS COSAS...CON "ELLOS" Y "NOSOTROS"

Iskra, mama je rekla da brod smrdi, a ne Albanci! Brod je prljav, i zato smrdi!

A mama… imaju li Albanci redove?

Albanci su ljudi kao mi Iskra!

Iskra, Mom said that the boat stank, not the Albanians! The boat is dirty, so it stinks!

Say, Mom ... do Albanians have a queue?

Albanians are people like us, Iskra!

ISKRA, MAMÁ DIJO QUE EL BARCO APESTABA, NO LOS ALBANESES! ¡EL BARCO ESTÁ SUCIO, ASÍ QUE APESTA!

¿DIME, MAMÁ ...TIENEN LOS ALBANESES UNA COLA?

¡LOS ALBANESES SON GENTE COMO NOSOTROS, ISKRA!

Boomtown Love

Matthew Robinson

In the hills of the high desert, while lost and careless and probably a little drunk, you stumble across a vein of gold, break out your pickaxe and go to frantic work chipping and hacking out a space large enough to fit into.

It's just big enough, except the fragments you pull out in ragged fists with bloodied knuckles, instead of throwing them out to make room for yourself, you pack your fucking pockets with them. Pants pockets, vest pockets, balled up in your cheeks like a dense plug of tobacco. With these remnants of this busted vein pushing out at your seams, you try to squeeze in.

It's too tight.

So you swing the pickaxe and make some room. And the piece goes into a pocket and nothing has changed except the hole is bigger.

The realization happens: this is what it means to strike gold, always digging and pocketing and toiling. So you call out, "Eureka, gold!"

Boomtown ást

Matthew Robinson

(Þýtt úr Ensku, Michael Lohr)

Í fjöllunum í háum eyðimörkinni, en glatað og kærulaus og líklega lítið drukkinn, hrasir þú yfir bláæð af gulli, brjótast út hirðinn þinn og fer í hrikalegt vinnuflæði og hakk út pláss sem er nógu stór til að passa inn í.

Það er bara nógu stórt, nema brotin sem þú dregur út í rauðum hnefa með blóðugum hnúfum, í stað þess að kasta þeim út til að gera pláss fyrir þig, pakkarðu föstum vasa með þeim. Buxur vasar, vestur vasa, balled upp í kinnum þínum eins og þétt tappi tóbaks.

Með þessum leifum af þessum busted æð ýta út á saumana þína, reynir þú að kreista inn. Það er of þétt.

Þannig að þú sveiflar hirðinn og gerir eitthvað pláss. Og verkið fer í vasa og ekkert hefur breyst nema holan sé stærri.

Framkvæmdin gerist: Þetta er það sem það þýðir að slá gull, alltaf að grafa og pocketing og toiling. Svo þú hringir út, "Eureka, gull!"

Þú klappir óhreinum höndum þínum yfir munninn þinn, hræddur

Kad žila presahne

Matthew Robinson
(Prijevod Ana Katana)

Dok bauljaš brežuljcima kalifornijske pustinje, izgubljen, sam, neobuzdan i vjerojatno djelomično pijan, nalijećeš na zlatnu žilu. Sučeš pijuk i manijakalno se bacaš na komadanje i krčenje ne bi li iskopao prostor dovoljno širok da staneš u nj.

Taman ti je dovoljno širok, samo što komade koje izranjavanim šakama i krvavim člancima vadiš i trpaš u vlastite jebene džepove, umjesto da ih izbaciš van. Džepove hlača, džepove prsluka, nabijaš ih kao duhan u obraze. Samog sebe, natrpanog ostacima iskopane rupe, pokušavaš nabiti u tu rupu.

Preusko ti je.

Laćaš se pijuka i praviš si mjesta. Trpaš otkinuti komad u džep i ništa se ne mijenja, osim što je rupa veća.

Tad shvaćaš, tako je to kad naletiš na zlato, stalno kopaš, trpaš u džepove, nabijaš i mučiš se.

"Eureka, zlato", povičeš.

Poklapaš si usta prljavim dla-

Amor Boomtown

Matthew Robinson
(traducción, T. Warburton y Bajo y rvb)

En las colinas del alto desierto, mientras andas perdido y sin cuidado y probablemente algo borracho, encuentras una vena de oro, sacas tu pico y comienzas a cavar frenéticamente, tajando un espacio lo suficientemente grande para caber adentro.

Es lo suficientemente grande, excepto por los fragmentos que sacas en puños machacados con nudillos ensangrentados, en vez de tirarlos para hacerte espacio, llenas tus pinches bolsillos con ellos. Bolsillos del pantalón, bolsillos del chaleco, hechos bola en tus cachetes como un denso tapón de tabaco. Con éstos restos de ésta vena rota empujándote las costuras, intentas entrar.

Está muy apretado.

Así que oscilas tu pico y haces algo de espacio. Y pones la pieza en un bolsillo y nada ha cambiado excepto que el hoyo es más grande.

La realización ocurre: ésto es lo que significa encontrar oro, siempre escarbando y embolsillando y esforzándo. Así que gritas, "¡Eureka, oro!"

Aplaudes tus manos sucias sobre tu boca, temiendo que alguien oiga,

You clap your dirty hands over your mouth, afraid that someone will hear, will come running with their own goddamn pickaxe and follow the vein further up and dig their own too-small hole and truncate the vein, cutting off the source. But your hands get there too late, and there are nuggets of dull yellow in them and the sound gets out and it follows the hillside and canyon walls and the wind carries what it can until it is heard and the boom comes.

It looks, when it comes, it looks like salvation, a brigade of pickaxe wielders sleeping in an organized array of tents until you find the tenacity to fell the few trees in sight and put up a store and a brothel and a church. You dig and drink and fuck and fucking dig.

You ride out with overflowing pockets and saddlebags, to cash in because of course gold is worthless until it's weighed and priced. You come back and return to the work, but what you took is gone; you start a new hole.

It's heavy work, day in and day out. This work is murder. People die doing it. A busted knuckle. Later, infection. A collapsed shaft with splintered beams. Glintless dark. Suffocating. Burst heart muscle from the goddamn strain. When the first one falls over, after you relieve them of their lode, you construct a fence around the top of a nearby hill, leaving one

um að einhver muni heyra, munu koma í gangi með eigin gömlu hirðinum sínum og fylgja bláæðinu lengra upp og grafa sjálfan sig líka lítið gat og styttu bláæðina og skera upp uppsprettuna. En hendur þínar komast of seint og það eru litla steina af daufa gula í þeim og hljóðið kemur út og það fylgir hlíðinni og gljúfrum veggjum og vindurinn ber það sem það getur þar til það heyrist og bómullinn kemur.

Þegar það kemur, lítur það út á hjálpræði. Stórfylki velja öxi notendur raða sig í fjölda tjalda fyrir nóttina. Í dögun dreifast þeir úr búðunum í burstann, leita kröfu þeirra, bölvast við vinnu og óhreinindi og hvert annað, hlaupa í gegnum vistir og tala um að fara heim. Það er, þangað til þú finnur þrautseigjan að fella fáein tré í augum og setja upp búð og handbolta og kirkju.

Þú grafa og drekka og ríða og ríða dig.

Þú rennur út með barmafullum vasa og hnakkapoka til reiðufé í því að auðvitað er gull einskis virði þar til það er vegið og verðlagað. Þú kemur aftur og kemur aftur til vinnu, en það sem þú tókst er farinn; þú byrjar nýtt gat.

Það er mikil vinna, dagur inn og dagur út. Þessi vinna er morð. Fólk deyr að gera það. Særður hné. Seinna, sýking.

A hrynja bol með brotinn geislar. Glanslaust dökk. Kæfa. Springa hjartavöðva úr guðsþrýstingnum. Þegar fyrsti maður fellur yfir, eftir að þú hefur létta þeim af

nom, jer strahuješ da će te netko čuti i dotrčati s vlastitim prokletim pijukom, i slijediti žilu još dalje, iskopati vlastitu premalu rupu, zagušiti žilu, prekinuti dotok.

No dlanovi ti nije dovoljno brzi. Puni su zagasito žutog grumenja i zvuk se pronosi niz obronak i kanjon i vjetar sa sobom nosi sve što može dok ga svi ne čuju i malo zatim stiže udar.

Isprva djeluje poput spasenja. Brigada naoružana pijucima postavlja šatore za noće. Zorom napuštaju logor i nestaju u šipražju, tražeći ono što im pripada, proklinjući ovu muku, prljavštinu i jedni druge, trošeći zalihe i razgovarajući o povratku kući. Sve do trenutka kad smogneš snage oboriti ono malo drveća što ima, podignuti trgovinu, javnu kuću i crkvu. Kopaš, piješ, jebeš i opet jebeno kopaš.

Odjahao si prepunjenih džepova i nabreklih bisaga jer svi znaju da je zlato bezvrijedno prije vaganja i procjene. Vraćaš se natrag, primaš se posla, ali nema više onoga što si odnio; kopaš novu rupu. Težak je to rad, iz dana u dan. Pravo ubojstvo. Ljudi zbilja umiru od toga. Raskrvaren članak, pa infekcija. Urušeno okno, raznesene grede. Mrak kao u rogu. Bez ikakva sjaja. Gušenje. Srčani mišić prepukao od prokletog napora. Kada prvi padne, nakon što ga riješite tereta, gradite ogradu

que vengan corriendo con su propio maldito pico y sigan la vena más arriba y caven su propio pequeño agujero y trunquen la vena, cortando la fuente. Pero tus manos llegan demasiado tarde, y hay trozos de amarillo opaco en ellas y el sonido se escapa y sigue la ladera y paredes del cañón y el viento acarrea lo que puede hasta que es escuchado y el auge llega.

Parece, cuando llega, como una salvación, una brigada de trabajadores empuñando picos durmiendo en un organizado conjunto de tiendas de campaña hasta que encuentras la tenacidad para talar los pocos árboles que hay a la vista y para establecer tienda. Burdel. Iglesia.

Excavas. Bebes. Jodes. Y excavas a la jodida.

Cabalgas con bolsillos y alforjas desbordantes, para cobrar en efectivo porque el oro es inútil hasta que haya sido pesado y valorado. Regresas y vuelves al trabajo, pero lo que te llevaste se ha ido; empiezas un nuevo hoyo.

Es trabajo duro, día a día. Este trabajo es matón. Gente muere haciéndolo. Un nudillo roto. Más tarde, infección. Un pozo de mina colapsado con vigas astilladas. Un oscuro sin destello. Asfixiante. Músculos cardíacos que se revientan por el maldito esfuerzo. Cuando el primero cae muerto, después de relevarlo de su carga, construyes una valla alrededor de la cumbre de una colina

graceful tree to mark the cemetery from a distance. Over time you bury the dead with calming regularity, the tree looking down at the sharp markers of stone you inscribe and set and level.

Then this: you lose the line of gold. Your pickaxe finds only rocky soil and sandy soil and bedrock and heartbreak. You turn around to retrace your steps but behind, you've chipped away everything between the holes, carried it off, leaving an empty rut.

You pack up and leave. You take your tent and your wooden church and your now-dull pickax and ride on.

Sometimes you think you left something, dropped while digging. In the quiet dark you think about coming back to poke around and maybe find out what you lost. But you would find only a tree looking down on an organized array of worn rock with unreadable epitaphs, surrounded by a failing fence. *Q*

lode þeirra, reisir þú girðing um toppinn í nærliggjandi hæð og skilur eitt tignarlegt tré til að merkja kirkjugarðinn í fjarlægð. Með tímanum gröfir þú hina dauðu með róandi regluleysi, tréið lítur niður á skarpa strik af steini sem þú skrifar og setur og stigi.

Þá þetta: þú missir línuna af gulli. Pickaxe þín finnur aðeins rokkandi jarðveg og sandur jarðveg og berggrunn og hjartsláttur.

Þú snýr aftur til að endurfæra skref þitt en aftan hefur þú flutt allt á milli gatanna, borið það burt og skilið tómt rif.

Þú pakkar upp og fer. Þú tekur tjaldið þitt og trékirkjuna þína og nú kyrrlátur velja öxi þinn og ríður á.

Stundum telur þú að þú skiljir eitthvað, sleppt meðan þú grófst. Í rólegu dimmunni hugsarðu um að koma aftur til að kippa í kring og kannski komast að því sem þú misstir. En þú myndir finna aðeins tré að horfa niður á skipulögðu fjölbreytta borið rokk með ólæsilegum epitaphs, umkringdur gallalaus girðing. *Q*

oko vrha obližnjeg brda, ostavljajući tamo jedno milostivo drvo kao znak groblja vidljiv izdaleka. Kako vrijeme prolazi, mrtvi se pokapaju u smirujući,. pravilnim razmacima. Krošnja drveta gleda dolje ka oštrim kamenim biljezima koje živi ispisuju, postavljaju i poravnavaju.

Zatim dolazi sljedeće: gubiš zlatnu žilu. pijuk ti nalijeće samo na kamenito tlo, pjeskovito tlo, stijenje i razočaranje. Okrećeš se ne bi li se vratio unatrag istim putem, no sve si raskomadao, raznio, prodao. Ostala ti je samo prazna jama.

Kupiš stvari i odlaziš. Sklapaš svoj šator, drvenu crkvu, otupjeli pijuk i jašeš dalje.

Ponekad pomisliš da ti je nešto ostalo, možda je ispalo tijekom kopanja. U tišini mraka razmišljaš o povratku, da malo pročačkaš i možda pronađeš izgubljeno.

No dočekalo bi te samo drvo koje gleda dolje na pravilno posloženo kamenje puno nečitljivih epitafa, okruženo ogradom koja posustaje. Q

cercana, dejando un árbol grácil para marcar el cementerio desde la distancia. Con el tiempo entierras a los muertos con una regularidad calmante, el árbol vigilando los agudos marcadores de piedra que inscribes y fijas y nivelas.

Luego ésto: pierdes la línea de oro. Tu pico solamente encuentra suelo rocoso y arenoso y lecho de roca y angustia. Te giras para rastrear tus pasos pero detrás, has astillado todo entre los hoyos, y te lo has llevado, dejando solo un surco vacío.

Empacas y te vas. Te llevas tu tienda de campaña y tu iglesia de madera y tu pico ya mellado y te marchas.

A veces piensas que dejaste algo, que se te cayó mientras cavabas. En la quietud oscura piensas en regresar para buscar y tal vez encontrar lo que perdiste. Pero sólo encontrarías un árbol vigilando un organizado conjunto de piedras desgastadas con epitafios ilegibles, rodeadas por una valla fallida. Q

Human Conditional: A Triptych

1. An Unsettled Script

Exhilarated. Vast of head. He fell out
with the world as it had to be.
From one version of "be" to the next:
the blossom falls from the tree. It must.
The musk of it. Oil needs changing. Music
from an open door is nobody's invitation.
He smoked a cigarette and watched the shadows play.
If the tanks arrive, at least he can fight –
meanwhile, there is work to be done.
Nothing – – –
can make up for the time that is lost.
(If only I could get out of this scene.) He wants
to walk the streets alone, find water,
gaze at glitter in sultry ink. Think.

2. The Immaculate Escape

To think is to walk in the sand, he said,
the ground giveth and it taketh away.
Vast empires of mind are built this way,
sinking with time, flooding, like Venice.
But to dive in is to enter a flux without end,
exhilarating as it might be. The way out
is the way in, perfect moments be damned.
Our hero sits down to smoke on the strand.
The late sun casts him in bronze. Seagulls
take no heed. A city looms over his shoulder again
with its pallid grid of responsibility and sin.
He knows: these are the adjectives we give ourselves
for the privilege of our society. He burps.
He farts. He feels numb with the evening star.

3. Provisional Uncertainty

Someone had to die to know what must be done.
We take our cues from corpses, or hide
in a wilderness of information, imbibing

Žmogaus būklinis: Triptikas

Neaiškus scenarijus

Įsismaginęs. Galvos platybėse. Jis susiriejo
su pasauliu, tokiu, koks ir turėjo būti.
Nuo vienos „būti" versijos ligi kitos:
žiedas krenta nuo medžio. Privalo kristi.
Jis kvepia muskusu. Tepalus reikia keisti. Muzika,
sklindanti pro atviras duris, yra niekieno kvietimas.
Jis sutraukė cigaretę ir stebėjo šešėlių žaismą.
Jei atvažiuos tankai, jis bent jau galės kautis –
o iki tol – yra darbo.
Niekas ---
neatlygins už laiką, kuris buvo prarastas.
(Jei tik pavyktų ištrūkt iš šios scenos.) Jis nori
vienas vaikščioti gatvėmis, susirast vandens,
žvelgt į gašliai žibantį rašalą. Mąstyt.

Nekaltas pabėgimas

Mąstyti reiškia žengti smėliu, tarė jis,
žemė duoda, žemė atima.
Šitaip iškyla didžiulės imperijos,
skęstant, grimztant išvien su laiku, lyg Venecija.
Nerti reiškia įžengti į begalinį srautą,
galbūt įkvepiantį. Durys lauk yra
durys vidun, tebūnie prakeiktos tobulos akimirkos.
Mūsų herojus prisėda parūkyt pakrantėj.
Pavakario saulė užlieja jį bronza. Žuvėdros
nekreipia dėmesio. Per petį jam vėl šmėkšteli miesto
blankus atskomybės ir nuodėmės tinklas.
Jis žino: tai būdvardžiai, kuriuos suteikiam patys sau
už visuomenines privilegijas. Jis atsirūgia.
Jis nusiperdžia. Jis nustėra, išvydęs žvaigždę vakarę.

Laikinas netikrumas

Kažkas turėjo mirt, kad sužinotų, kas privalo būt padaryta.
Naudojamės lavonų užuominom arba slepiamės
informacijos tyruose, suryjam tai, kas laivai

Ljudski kondicional: Triptih

1. Nejasan scenarij

Uzbuđenost. Beskraj u glavi. Posvadio se
sa svijetom kao što i treba.
Od jedne inačice „biti" do druge:
cvijeće opada s drveća. Mora.
Mošusni miris. Treba promijeniti ulje. Glazba
s otvorenih vrata ničija je pozivnica.
Pušio je cigaretu i gledao igru sjena.
Stignu li tenkovi, barem se može boriti –
u međuvremenu, ima posla.
Ništa – – –
ne može nadoknaditi izgubljeno vrijeme.
(Da bar mogu izbaciti taj prizor.) Želi
sam hodati ulicama, pronaći vodu,
zuriti u svjetlucanje sparne tinte. Misliti.

2. Nevin bijeg

Misliti jest hodati pijeskom, rekao je,
tlo daje i uzima.
Silna carstva uma tako se grade,
tonu s vremenom, poplavljuju, poput Venecije.
No roniti jest ući u beskrajan tijek,
ma koliko uzbudljivo bilo. Izlaz
jest ulaz, k vragu sa savršenim trenucima.
Naš junak sjedne zapaliti na plaži.
Kasno sunce obasjava ga broncom. Galebovi
se ne obaziru. Grad mu se opet nadvija nad ramenom
blijedom mrežom odgovornosti i grijeha.
Zna: to su pridjevi koje si pridajemo
zbog privilegija našega društva. Podrigne.
Prdne. Otupi do prve večernje zvijezde.

3. Provizorna nesigurnost

Netko je morao umrijeti da se zna što treba.
Primamo naputke od leševa, ili se skrivamo
u divljini informacija, upijajući

Humano Condicional: Un Tríptico

1. Una escritura inquieto

Excitado. Enorme de cabeza. Reñio
con el mundo como tenía que ser.
De una versión de "ser" a la siguiente:
la flor cae del árbol. Debe hacerlo.
El almizcle. El aceite necesita cambiarse. La música
de una puerta abierta no invita a nadie.
Fumó un cigarrillo y vio el juego de sombras.
Si los tanques llegan, al menos él puede luchar –
Mientras tanto, hay trabajo por hacer.
Nada – – –
puede compensar el tiempo perdido.
(Si solamente yo pudiera salir de esta escena.) Él quiere
andar las calles solo, encontrar agua,
mirar el brillo en tinta bochornosa. Pensar.

2. La Inmaculada Escapar

Pensar es caminar en la arena, dijo,
el suelo le da y la quita.
Vastos imperios de la mente se construyen de esta manera,
hundiéndose con el tiempo, inundaciones, como Venecia.
Pero sumergirse en es entrar en un flujo sin fin,
estimulante como podría ser. La escotilla de escape
es la entrada real, al infierno con los momentos perfectos.
Nuestro héroe se sienta a fumar en la playa.
El sol de crepúsculo lo lanza en bronce. Las gaviotas
no le prestan atención. Una ciudad de nuevo se cierne sobre
su hombro
con su pálida rejilla de responsabilidad y pecado.
Sabe: éstos son los adjetivos que nos damos
por el privilegio de nuestra sociedad. Eructa.
Se pede. Se siente entumecido con la estrella vespertina.

3. Incertidumbre Provisional

Alguien tuvo que morir para saber qué hacer.
Tomos nuestras señales de cadáveres, o nos escondemos
en un desierto de información, bebiendo

what floats freely in the clouds, like lunch.
But there is a mustiness to every must
that reaches the sensitive nose. Hold up! –
An animal has passed by. Drops of fur
darken the concrete floor. Has anyone
brought an umbrella? One man strides
with his head held high, drinking the rain
of beasts – a tiger stuffed in a suit and tie.
He dreams of throwing off his shoes
as he did as a child, strewing the lawn
with the petals of his feet. He too must die.

— *Rimas Uzgiris*

plūduriuoja debesuos, kaip pietus.
Bet kiekvienas „privalau“ turi savo privalomybę,
kuri kutena jautrią uoslę. Sustok –
Gyvūnas praėjo pro šalį. Kailio gniutulai
užtemdo betonines grindis. Gal kas
atsinešė skėtį? Vienišas vyras žengia
galva iškelta, gerdamas lietų žvėrių –
tigras, įspraustas į kostiumą.
Jis svajoja nusispirt batus
kaip vaikystėj, kai barstė savo pėdų
žiedlapius po veją. Jis taip pat turi mirti.

— *Rimas Uzgiris*
(Iš anglų kalbos vertė Dominykas Norkūnas)

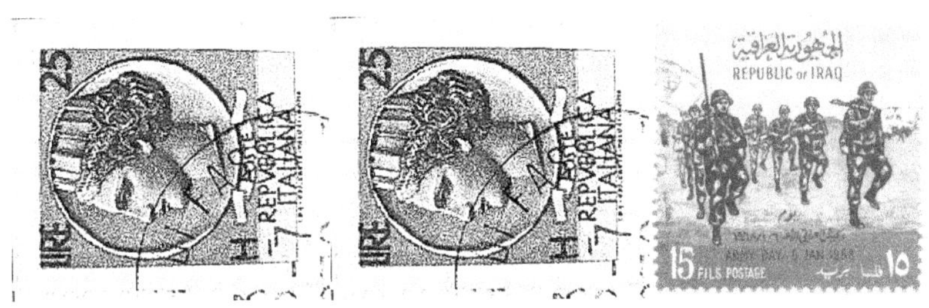

ono što slobodno lebdi u oblacima, poput ručka.
No svako „moram" ima svoju odgovornost,
koja draška osjetljiv nos. Stani! –
Prošla je životinja. Krzno
pomrači beton. Je li tko
ponio kišobran? Jedan čovjek hoda
uzdignute glave, pijući kišu
zvijeri - tigar u odijelu i s kravatom.
Sanja o tome da odbaci cipele
kao dijete, da laticama svojih stopala
zaspe travnjak. I on mora umrijeti.

— *Rimas Uzgiris*
(Prijevod, Jelena Pataki)

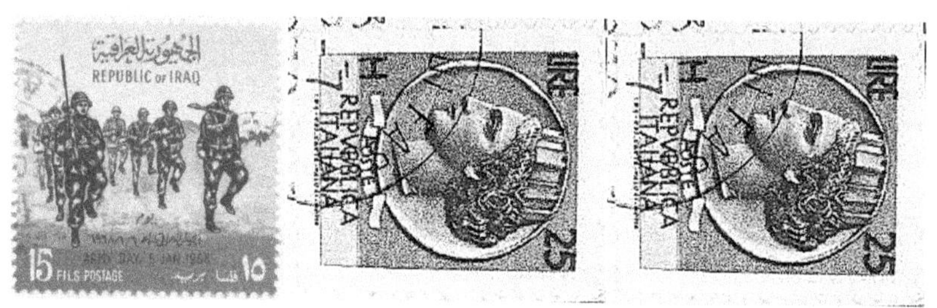

lo que flota libremente en las nubes, como almuerzo.
Pero hay algo almizcleño a cada almizcle
que alcanza a la nariz sensible. ¡Espere! –
Un animal ha pasado. Gotas de piel
oscurezcan el piso de hormigón. ¿Alguien ha
traído un paraguas? Un hombre anda a trancos
con su cabeza bien alto, bebiendo la lluvia
de bestias, un tigre metido en un traje y corbata.
Sueña con quitarse los zapatos
como lo hizo cuando era niño, esparciendo el césped
con los pétalos de sus pies. También debe morir.

— *Rimas Uzgiris*
(Traducción, T. Warburton y Bajo y rvb)

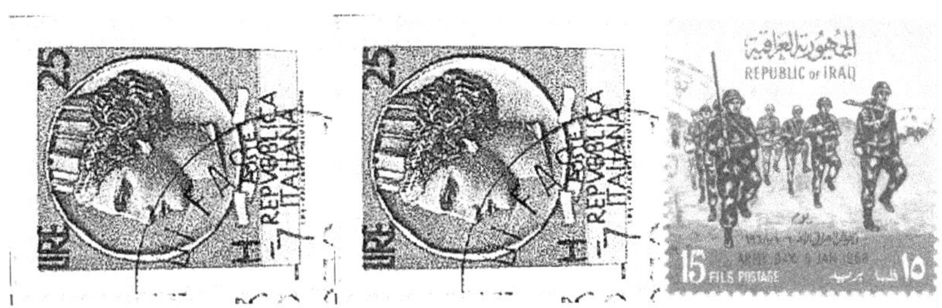

O OLOVCI

O svemu je, čini se, lakše pisati nego o običnoj olovci.
Naime, olovka živi od vlastita nestajanja.
Dok u čaši besposlena stoji, nje zapravo nema,
mjesto nje neko pougljenjeno drvce svoj posao uzalud čeka.
Kada ju u ruke uzme petogodišnja djevojčica,
olovka ju odmah razumije i potpuno joj se preda.
Priđe joj bez straha, pusti da se crnilo iz olovke na papir prospe.
Dok crta, pod njezinim se prstima topi tanko tijelo olovke
i uz tiho struganje po papiru rađaju se stabla bez korijenja,
zmajevi, mećave zvijezda, papučice s trepetljikama.
Ako je Sir Walter Raleigh mogao izvagati dim,
tko bi mogao izvagati srce olovke?
Je li crnilo na papiru jednako težini njezina srca?
A ako olovkom crta dijete, i na papir prosipa crnilo,
je li i njegovo srce već pomalo crno da olovci se daje?

— Miroslav Kirin

ABOUT THE PENCIL

Of everything, it seems, is easier to write than of an ordinary pencil.
Namely, the pencil lives off its own disappearance.
While it idly sits in a cup, it doesn't really exist,
instead a charred out piece of wood in vain awaits its task.
When taken into the hands of a five-year old girl,
the pencil understands at once and surrenders to her completely.
Without fear it approaches her, letting the black graphite spill onto paper.
While she draws, the thin pencil body melts under her fingers
as from the quiet scratching on the paper emerge rootless trees,
dragons, whirlwinds of stars, ciliate paramecia
If Sir Walter Raleigh was capable of weighing smoke,
who could weigh the heart of a pencil?
Is the black on the paper equal to the weight of its heart?
And if a child draws with a pencil, spilling the blackness onto paper,
isn't its heart surrendering to a pencil also already slightly black?

— *Miroslav Kirin*
(Tr. fr. the Croatian, Boris Gregorić)

À propos du crayon

Tout est plus facile, me semble-t-il, que d'écrire à propos d'un simple
crayon.
En effet un crayon vit de sa propre disparition.
Tant qu'il reste désœuvré dans un verre, il n'existe pas vraiment,
à sa place une brindille carbonisée attend en vain son travail.
Quand une fillette de cinq ans le prend dans les mains,
le crayon la comprend tout de suite et s'adonne entièrement.
Elle l'approche sans peur, elle laisse sa noirceur de crayon
se déverser sur le papier.
Pendant qu'elle dessine, le corps fin du crayon
fond sous ses doigts et dans un doux grattage sur le papier naissent des
arbres sans racines,
des dragons, des tempêtes d'étoiles, des paramécies.
Si Sir Walter Raleigh pouvait peser la fumée,
qui pourrait peser le cœur du crayon?
La noirceur sur le papier a-t-elle le même poids que son cœur?
Et si c'est un enfant qui dessine au crayon, et verse
la noirceur sur le papier,
son cœur n'est-il pas déjà un peu noir
pour s'adonner au crayon?

— *Miroslav Kirin*
(traduit par Martina Kramer)

Sobre el lápiz

Es más fácil escribir sobre todo, parece, que escribir sobre un lápiz ordinario.
Es decir, el lápiz vive de su propia desaparición.
Mientras se sienta ociosamente en una taza, no existe realmente,
en su lugar un pedazo de madera carbonizados en vano espera su tarea.
Cuando se toma en las manos de una niña de cinco años,
el lápiz entiende en una vez y se rinde a ella por completo.
Sin miedo se acerca a ella, dejando que el grafito negro se derrame en el papel.
Mientras ella dibuja, el delgado cuerpo del lápiz delgado se derrite bajo sus dedos,
ya que de su quieto rasguño en el papel emergen árboles sin raíces,
dragones, torbellinos de estrellas, Paramecia ciliada
Si el señor Walter Raleigh era capaz de pesar el humo,
¿quién podría pesar el corazón de un lápiz?
¿Iguala el negro en el papel al peso de su corazón?
Y si un niño dibuja con un lápiz, derramando la oscuridad sobre el papel,
¿no está rendiéndose su corazón a un lápiz ya también un poco negro?

— *Miroslav Kirin*
(Traducción, T. Warburton y Bajo y rvb)

SUMMER FEELS

miglė anušauskaitė

VASAROS JAUSMAI

Iš anglų kalbos vertė,
miglė anušauskaitė

SUMAR FİNNST

Þýtt úr Ensku,
Michael Lohr

ljetno doba

Prijevod,
Jelena Pataki

verano siente

Traducción,
T. Warburton y Bajo y rvb

Man patinka matyti saulės atspindžius ant
blakstienų, kai primerkiu akis.

Ég elska að sjá sólgleraugu
Á augnhárum myndir
Þegar ég hálf loka augum mínum.

OBOŽAVAM VIDJETI SUNČEV ODRAZ
NA SVOJIM TREPAVICAMA KADA NAPOLA
ZAŽMIRIM

ME ENCANTA VER REFLEJOS SOLARES
EN MIS PESTAÑAS
CUANDO ENTRECIERRO MIS OJOS.

I REMEMBER SEEING THEM
AS A KID.

I WONDER IF I WILL ALWAYS
BE ABLE TO SEE THEM.

Atsimenu, kaip stebėdavau juos, kai buvau maža.

Ég man eftir að sjá þá
sem krakki.

SJEĆAM SE DA SAM GA VIDJELA
KAO DIJETE

ME ACUERDO DE VERLOS
CUANDO ERA NIÑA.

Įdomu, ar visada galėsiu juos matyti.

Ég vona að ég vili alltaf
veita að gera að sía.

PITAM SE HOĆU LI GA UVIJEK
MOĆI VIDJETI

ME PREGUNTO SI YO SIEMPRE
PODRÉ VERLOS.

OR WHEN I'M WALKING
ON A SUMMER NIGHT
AND THE AIR IS JUST
SO SATURATED

AND SUDDENLY I STEP
INTO A
SPACE
-A POCKET-
OF FRESH AIR.

Arba kai vasaros naktį kur nors eini ir oras toks prisotintas ir staiga įžengiu į gaivaus oro erdvę — tarsi kišenę.

Eða eða gangur á sumar. Nótt Og loftið er bara það saturð
Og stundum hef ég stíga í a rúm —eð vasa— Af ferskum lofti.

ILI KADA ŠEĆEM ZA LJETNE NOĆI A ZRAK JE TOLIKO GUST PA ODJEDNOM ZAKORAČIM U PROSTOR — DŽEP — SVJEŽEG ZRAKA.

O CUANDO ANDE DURANTE UNA NOCHE DE VERA-
NO Y EL AIRE ESTÉ TAN SATURADO
Y DE REPENTE ANDE EN UN ESPACIO — UN BOLSILLO
— DE AIRE FRESCO.

Jaučiuosi, tarsi būčiau palietusi kažką milžiniško ir nesuprantamo, ir abejingo. Jaučiuosi lyg palaiminta.

Mér finnst eins og ég hef bara rétt eitthvað mikil og
Óhjákvæmilegt og óbreytt.

Mér finnst blessað.

IMAM OSJEĆAJ DA SAM UPRAVO DODIRNULA NEŠTO GOLEMO I NESHVATLJIVO I RAVNODUŠNO. OSJEĆAM SE BLAGOSLOVLJENO.

ME SIENTA COMO ACABO DE TOCAR ALGO ENORME E
INCOMPRENSIBLE E INDIFERENTE.
ME SIENTA BENDECIDA.

BUT MY FAVOURITE THING MUST BE SUMMER SHOWERS.
WHEN EVERYTHING IS
FULL OF ANTICIPATION

AND SUDDENLY IT BREAKS OUT.
I FEEL SUCH A RUSH OF
INTENSE
DESTRUCTIVE
HAPPINESS

Bet mano mėgstamiausias dalykas turbūt yra vasaros liūtys. Kai viskas pripildyta laukimo

En, fjórirþjónustuð þinn skal skoða sommar Þegar allt er Fullt af neyðartilvikum

NO OMILJENI SU MI ZACIJELO LJETNI PLJUSKOVI KADA JE SVE PUNO IŠČEKIVANJA

PERO MI COSA FAVORITA DEBE SER LAS LLUVIAS DEVERANO. CUANDO TODO ESTÁ LLENO DE ANTICIPACIÓN

Ir staiga pasipila. Aš pajaučiu tokį stiprios destruktyvios laimės antplūdį

Og stundum fer það út. Mér finnst svona þjóta af ákafur eyðileggjandi hamingju

I ODJEDNOM SE PROLOMI. OSJEĆAM SILAN NALET SNAŽNE DESTRUKTIVNE SREĆE

Y DE REPENTE ESTALLA. SIENTO TAL AVALANCHA DE FELICIDAD DESTRUCTIVA INTENSA

I FEEL LIKE A SORT OF
ANCIENT PRE-MORAL BEING
THAT CREATES
AND
DESTROYS
OUT OF
SHEER AMUSEMENT.

Jaučiuosi kaip kokia senovinė iki-morali būtybė, kuri kuria ir naikina vien dėl pramogos.

Mér finnst eins og svartur af alþingi áður fyrrverandi Það skapar og Eyðileggur úr hreinn skemmtunar.

OSJEĆAMSEKAONEKOPRASTAROPREDMORALNO BIĆE KOJE STVARA I UNIŠTAVA RADI PUKE ZABAVE.

ME SIENTO COMO UNA DE UNA ESPECIE ANTIGUA Y PRE-MORAL QUE CREA Y DES-TRUYE POR PURA DIVERSIÓN.

Gerai, užtenka apie mano jausmus. Eikit... Eikit susi-rasti savo jausmų!

Allt í lagi, ekki umtilfinningarnar mínar. Getur ... getað þitt eigin tilfinning!

DOBRO, DOSTA O MOJIM OSJEĆAJIMA.IDI... IDI PO SVOJE OSJEĆAJE!

BIEN, BASTA DE MIS SENTIMIENTOS. VÉ... ¡VÉ A BUSCAR TUS PROPIOS SENTIMIENTOS!

WELL? GO! GET AWAY.

I'M A BIT EMBARRASSED OF HAVING TOLD YOU ALL THOSE THINGS.

Nu? Eikit! Eikit iš čia.

Vel? Fara! Komast burt.

NO? IDI ODLAZI?

¿BIEN? ¡VÉTE AHORA! ALÉJATE DE AQUÍ.

Man truputį gėda, kad aš čia tiek pripasakojau.

Ég er bitur stórkostleg hafa sagði þér allt þetta hlutir.

POMALO ME SRAM ŠTO SAM TI ISPRIČALA SVE TO.

ESTOY UN POCO AVERGONZADA POR HABERTE CONTADO TODAS ESAS COSAS.

Die Rückkehr des Odysseus

Nach Giorgio de Chirico

1

Das letzte Ruderstück besteht aus blauer Metaphysik.
Er paddelt auf dem Weltmeer im Wohnzimmer,
sitzt in seiner Nussschale auf dem Plüschteppich
und träumt vom Ende der Irrfahrt.

Ah, wie die See schäumt! Und erst die Götter –
wütend über den sterblichen Odysseus,
der wieder einmal allen ein Schnippchen schlägt
und jetzt sogar die Frechheit hat, so zu tun,
als würde er in der Badewanne sitzen und plantschen.
Was für ein durchtriebener Hund!

Aber wie immer weiss er ganz genau, was er macht.
Möglichst weit weg vom verführerisch lockenden Fauteuil!
Schnell ans ferne Ende der Teppichfransen!
Vorbei am tückischen Felsen des Wandschranks!
Dann ein Sprung auf das Festland der Dielen,
nicht auf den Bugholzstuhl und das offene Fenster
mit dem griechischen Tempel achten –
sondern ab durch die Tür ins Nebenzimmer!

2

Das alles, während er seine treulose Mannschaft
draussen auf dem Platz der beunruhigenden Musen
gegen einen Zweitligisten aus San Remo
oder Galatasaray Istanbul Fussball spielen
und wahrscheinlich verlieren lässt.

— *Clemens Umbricht*

The Return of Odysseus

After Giorgio de Chirico

1
The final passage by oars is made of blue metaphysic.
He paddles on the world-ocean in the living room,
sits in his nutshell on the plush carpet
and dreams of the end of his quest.

Ah, how the sea froths! And now the gods–
raging about the mortal Odysseus,
who once again played them all a trick
and even now had the insolence to do this,
as if he sat in the bathtub and splashed.
What a sly dog!

But as always he knows very well what he's doing.
Far away as possible from the seductive captivating armchair!
Swiftly to the end of the carpet fringe!
Past the treacherous crags of the armoire!
Then a leap to the continent of the hallway,
not to the bentwood chair and the open window
with a view of a Greek temple–
but out through the door into the next room!

2
While all this happens, his faithless crew
outside at the place of unsettling muses
play against a second rank team from San Remo
or Galatasaray Istanbul in soccer
and probably lose.

— *Clemens Umbricht*
(tr. Fr. The German, Douglas Spangle)

Povratak Odiseja

Nakon Giorgia de Chirica

1

Konačni prolaz veslima je napravljen od plave metafizike.
On vesla svijetom oceana u dnevnoj sobi,
sjedi u svojoj ljusci na plišanom tepihu
i sanja o kraju svoga traganja.

Ah, kako se more pijeni! I sada bogovi —
bijesne oko smrtnog Odiseja,
koji ih je još jednom izigrao
i čak je sada imao bezobrazluka to napraviti,
kao da sjedi u kadi i pršće.
Koji lukavac!

Ali kao i uvijek on jako dobro zna što radi.
Što dalje moguće od zavodljivog zanosnog naslonjača!
Brzo do kraja resa tepiha!
Poslije podmuklih grebena ormara!
Zatim skok do kontinenta hodnika,
ne do stolice od savijenog drveta i do
otvorenog prozora
s pogledom na grčki hram —
ali kroz vrata u sljedeću sobu!

2

Dok se sve ovo događa, njegova bespomoćna posada
vani na mjestu zabrinutih muza
igra protiv drugo rangirajuće momčadi iż San Rema
Ili Galatasaraya Istanbula u nogometu
i vjerojatno gubi.

— *Clemens Umbricht*
(Prijevod, Dijana Jakovac)

La vuelta de Odysseus

En homenaje a Giorgio de Chirico

1

el ultimo paso de remos está hecho de azul metafísico.
él rema bien en el mundo-océano en la sala,
se sienta en su cáscara de nuez sobre la afelpada alfombra
y sueña con final de su búsqueda.

¡ah, cómo se espuma el mar! y ahora los dioses —
rabiando por el mortal Odiseo,
que una vez más les hizo a todos un truco
e incluso ahora tuvo la insolencia de hacer esto,
como si se sentara en la bañera y chapoteara.
¡qué perro tan astuto!

pero como siempre, sabe muy bien lo que está haciendo.
¡tan lejos como sea posible del seductor y cautivador sillón!
¡rápidamente hacia la orilla del fleco de la alfombra!
¡más allá de los riscos traicioneros del armario!
y entonces, un salto al continente del pasillo,
no a la silla de madera curvada y la ventana abierta
con vista a un templo griego —
¡sino a través de la puerta hasta el siguiente cuarto!

2

mientras todo esto sucede, su infiel equipo
afuera en la plaza de las musas inquietantes
juega contra su equipo de fútbol de segundo rango de San
Remo
o de Galatasaray Estambul
y probablemente pierde.

— *Clemens Umbricht*
(traducción, T. Warburton y Bajo y rvb)

iLogue No. 39

(a conversation with Peter Turrini)

The rustle of your heart keeps me from falling asleep when I lay my head on your chest.
You see, Peter, day upon sacred day is wasted in the *quest for the justification of our mistrust.*
Recently you've become my confessor, the word I deny myself, the language I yell in
when I don't want to be understood.
It is a language of suffering and guilt, wide and deep enough to accomodate everything, as it has
stuffed multitudes into itself, only by batting
an eye.
As long as the quest is fruitless, we carry on, disappointed, the disappointment pushes us on and
deeper we dig and dig, wanting to find it.
I was telling you, Peter, and you refused to support me so I found even greater encouragement
in your reproach.
When I wanted to speed things up, I left for a few days, played truant, was,
somewhere I couldn't even explain to myself.
Which is good, not knowing where you were, with whom, having a crushing number of
uncertainties.
Luck is brought on by a sudden breach of trust.
The heart is a vibrating homeland bathed in blood that listens intently.
It whistled as it fell after us, into a ravaged center, *into the barren land amidst the weeds.*
We pass it on from hand to hand, as a red-hot orb.
Careful lest it slide from your hand, Peter, when you get up at night to take a piss.

— *Miroslav Kirin*
(tr. fr. the Croatian, Ana Katana)

Jalog br. 39

(razgovor s Peterom Turrinijem)

Ne mogu zaspati od šuma tvog srca kad pritisnem glavu na tvoja prsa.

Vidiš, Peter, baš svaki božji dan traje ta uporna *potraga za potvrdom našeg nepovjerenja.*

Odnedavna si moj ispovjednik, riječ koju si uskraćujem, jezik u koji vičem kad

ne želim da ga se razumije.

Jezik je to trpnje i krivnje, širok i dubok za sve, u se je potrpao mnoštva, tek treptajem

oka.

I sve dok je potraga jalova, mi razočarani nastavljamo, razočaranost nas tjera dalje i

dublje, rujemo i rujemo, želimo je naći.

Pripovijedao sam ti, Peter, nisi me želio podržati pa sam u tvojim prijekorima nalazio samo još veće ohrabrenje.

Kad sam htio da se sve ubrza, otišao bih nekamo na nekoliko dana, izbivao, bio, ali ni sebi poslije nisam mogao objasniti gdje.

Što je dobro, ne znati gdje si bio, s kim, što, imati slamajući broj neodređenosti.

Sreću donosi konačni slom povjerenja.

Srce je ustreptala gruda okupana krvlju koja napeto sluša.

Zviždeći je pala za nama, u izrovano središte, *u jalovinu među korovom.*

Prebacujemo ga iz ruke u ruku, kao usijanu kuglu.

Pazi da ti ne isklizne s dlana, Peter, kad noću ustaneš da ideš mokriti.

— *Miroslav Kirin*

Nulogue, n° 39

(discussion avec Peter Turrini)

Je ne peux m'endormir à cause du bruit de ton cœur
quand j'appuie ma tête contre ta poitrine.
Tu vois, Peter, cette persévérante *recherche de confirmation*
de notre méfiance se perpétue absolument chaque jour.
Depuis peu, tu es mon confesseur, la parole dont je me prive, la langue dans laquelle je crie quand
je ne veux pas qu'on la comprenne.
C'est la langue de l'endurance et de la culpabilité, large et profonde pour tout, elle s'est remplie des multitudes,
un clin
d'œil suffisait.
Et tant que la recherche n'a nullement avancé, nous persévérons déçus,
la déception nous pousse plus loin et plus profondément, nous
creusons et creusons, voulons la trouver.
Je te le racontais, Peter, tu ne voulais pas me soutenir, et dans tes remontrances
je trouvais
encore plus d'encouragements.
Quand je voulais tout accélérer, je partais quelque partpendant plusieurs jours, m'absentais, étais,
mais plus tard, je ne pouvais même pas m'expliquer où c'était.
Et c'est bien, de ne pas savoir où tu étais, avec qui, quoi, d'avoirun nombre d'indéterminations brisantes.
Le bonheur vient quand on brise définitivement la confiance.
Le cœur est une boule fébrile baignée dans le sang qui écoute attentivement.
Elle est tombée derrière nous en sifflant, au milieu d'un creux, *dans une terre infertile au milieu des mauvaises herbes*.
Nous le passons d'une main à l'autre, comme une boule ardente.
Attention de ne pas la faire glisser de ta paume, Peter, quand la nuit tu te lèveras pour aller uriner.

— Miroslav Kirin
(traduit par Vanda Mikšić)

miLogo núm. 39

(conversación con Pedro Turrini)

No me puedo dormir sobre el sonido de su latido del corazón mientras descanso
mi cabeza en su pecho.
Usted ve Pedro, *día tras día nos persistentemente buscamos la prueba de*
nuestra desconfianza.
Hace poco se hizo mi confesor, una expresión de la que me privo,
el idioma en que grito cuando no quiero ser entendido.
Es el idioma del sufrimiento y de la culpa, amplio y mas profundo para
acomodar a todo el mundo, se ha aborrado de multitudes, en un
mero parpadeo
de un ojo.
Así pues, mientras la búsqueda es infructuosa, seguimos,
decepcionados,
la desilusión nos empuja más lejos y
profundo, excavamos y excavamos, con intento de encontrarla.
Le he dicho esto muchas veces, Pedro, pero no ofrecería soporte así que
su reprimenda
sólo me animó aún más.
Cuando quería acelerarlo, iría a algún sitio por un par de días, me
gustaría estar lejos, me gustaría,
pero entonces no pude explicarme donde acababa de estar.
Lo que es bueno, no saber dónde estás, con quién estás, o qué, tener
un número aplastante de incertidumbres.
La derrota final de la confianza será la felicidad.
El corazón es un bulto temblando, bañado en la sangre, escuchando
seriamente.
Silbando, se ha caído detrás de nosotros, en el centro del hoyo, *en el*
terreno estéril cubierto de mala hierba.
Lo echamos de mano en mano, como una esfera candente.
Sólo no le dejes deslizarse hacia abajo la palma de su mano, Pedro,
cuando de noche despierta para mear.

— *Miroslav Kirin*
(traducción, T. Warburton y Bajo y rvb)

Jalog br. 41

Kad ti pogled zapne na košarici za kruh, ne diže se s nje satima, ondje ostaje kao na

mjestu

svog izbora, što dobro znam da nije.

Rekao bih da ne miruje posve, i ako sam dovoljno priseban

(što tad, dok joj ukočen pogled leži na košarici, nikako nisam) mogu zamijetiti kako

malo-pomalo prodire u košaricu, rastvara ju nizom protu-rečenica, što mi je posve

dovoljno (i nema veze s prisebnošću) da zakriljen drugom stranom zida počnem

snažno

stiskati obje šake tako da se nokti urežu u dlan i posiju novi svemir od polumjesecā.

Još malo jačim stiskom izbrišem cijeloga sebe, umotam se u nevidljivost.

Možda mi se dogodi da prikovanom pogledu vratim laganost, uletim u tvoje

lelujanje,

sad raspršeno u stvarima naglo oslobođenima prikovanosti,

i pomislim kako ljubav još nije počinjena.

— *Miroslav Kirin*

iLogue No. 41

When your eyes happen upon the bread basket they remain there for
hours, as if it were the
place
of their choice, which I well know it isn't.
I wouldn't say they're completely still, and if I'm thinking clearly
(which I'm not when her eyes lie still on the bread basket) I can
notice them
penetrate the basket,
little by little, deconstruct it with a series of
counter-sentences, which is just
fine by me (and has nothing to do with thinking clearly) because, as
I'm covered by the far side of the wall, I stare
intensely
tying both my fists so the nails make an entire
new universe of half-moons in the flesh of my palm.
I squeeze a little harder and completely erase myself, cloak myself in
invisibility.
I might just return the lightness to your petrified eyes,
I might just fly into your
private levitation,
dispersed among things unexpectedly
unchained,
thinking that love hasn't been committed yet.

— *Miroslav Kirin*
(translated fr. the Croatian, Ana Katana)

Nulogue n° 41

Quand ton regard s'arrête sur une corbeille à pain, ne la quitte plus pendant
des heures,
il s'y attarde comme sur
le lieu
de son choix, ce qu'elle n'est pas, je sais bien.
Je dirais qu'il ne reste pas sans bouger, et si j'ai suffisamment
de sang-froid (ce qui, pendant que son regard figé repose
sur la corbeille, n'est certainement pas le cas)
je peux noter que
petit à petit
il pénètre dans la corbeille, l'ouvre par une série de contre-propos,
ce qui me suffit parfaitement (et qui n'a rien à voir avec le sang-froid)
pour que, caché par un mur mitoyen, je me mette à serrer
fort
les deux poings en faisant s'enfoncer mes ongles dans mes paumes et semer
un nouvel univers fait de lunes croissantes.
En serrant plus fort encore, j'efface mon moi tout entier, et m'enveloppe
de l'invisibilité.
Il pourrait toujours m'arriver de rendre la légèreté à ton regard rivé,
d'être pris dans ton
ondoiement,
désormais dispersé dans les choses soudainement affranchies de fixité,
et de penser que l'amour n'a pas encore été commis.

— *Miroslav Kirin*
(traduit par Vanda Mikšić)

miLogo núm. 41

Cuando su mirada tropeza con la cesta de pan, permanece allí durante
    horas, como si
        fuera el lugar de su elección,
que sé bien no es.
No diría que sus ojos están totalmente en reposo, y si estoy
    suficientemente cuerdo
(cuando sus ojos están remachados en la cesta, no soy en
absoluto de eso) voy a notar que tu mirada
        penetre la canasta, tan lentamente, lo rompe
abierto con una cadena de anti-afirmaciones,
que es todo lo que necesito (y no tiene nada que hacer con la cordura)
    porque estoy refugiado detrás del otro lado de la pared
y empiezo a apretar mis puños
tan intensamente
que mis uñas cavan en mis palmas y imprimen en ellos
un cosmos completamente nuevo de medias lunas.
Si los aprieto un poco más, yo me borro completamente,
me encubro mismo en la invisibilidad.
Quizás traeré la ingravidez a tu mirada fija,
        te acompañaré en tu levitación,
ahora me camuflaré entre las cosas abruptamente desencadenadas,
y me parece a mí, el amor todavía no se ha cometido.

— *Miroslav Kirin*
(tradducíon, T. Warburton y Bajo y rvb)

Jalog br 42

U već klasičnom japanskom filmu gorski zdenac skriva žrtvu ljubavnog prekršaja. Daleko je od radoznalih očiju, od mrmljavog svijeta, no nikad predaleko i naposljetku se nedozivane oči ipak pojave i ono što je htjelo biti potisnuto i skriveno izranja na njegovu površinu.

Usred prostrana dvorišta muzeja Louvre staklena kupola skriva jedan takav zdenac, zapravo podzemne prostorije muzeja u kojima je knjižara i suvenirnica. Kao da muzej želi što duže zadržati svoje posjetioce, pa i zatočiti ih.

Spušta se bijela pariška noć koja počinje tek poslije deset uvečer. Iscrpljeni, sjedamo na rub što kružno opšiva staklenu kupolu i u taj nas čas zabljesne svjetlost s dna kupole. Načas smo obnevidjeli, ali kad bistrina ponovno ovlada našim očima, zamijetimo mladu Japanku na samome dnu toga presahnulog zdenca. I čini nam se da nam maše. Razdragana je: upravo nas je zatočila na svojoj fotografiji.

— *Miroslav Kirin*

iLog No 42

In a Japanese movie that's recently become a classic, a mountain well hides the victim of a crime of passion. She's hidden away, far from the chattering crowd, but never far enough, and eventually uninvited eyes appear. Everything that was meant to be hidden and suppressed springs to the surface of the well.

The spacious courtyard dome of the Louvre hides an almost identical well. The subterranean halls and the museum souvenir shop are in it. As if the museum wanted to keep its visitors as long as possible, imprison them even.

A white Parisian night falls upon us, springing to life only after ten. Exhausted, we sit on the circular edge surrounding the glass dome. All of a sudden, a light shines from the bottom. We're blinded for a moment, but when clarity reappears, we spot a young Japanese woman at the bottom of that dried-up well. It seems as if she were waving to us. She's delighted; she has imprisoned us within her snapshot.

— *Miroslav Kirin*
(tr. fr. the Croatian, Ana Katana)

Nulogue, n° 42

Dans un film japonais devenu classique, un puits dans la montagne dissimule la victime d'un amour interdit. Loin des regards curieux, du monde marmonnant, mais jamais assez loin, et à la fin, les yeux qu'on n'a pas conviés apparaissent tout de même et ce qui voulait être refoulé et dissimulé fait surface.

Au milieu de la cour spacieuse du musée du Louvre, la pyramide de verre cache ce genre de puits, en réalité l'espace souterrain du musée abritant une libraire et un magasin de souvenirs. Comme si le musée voulait retenir le plus longtemps possible ses visiteurs, et même les confiner.

La nuit blanche parisienne tombe, elle qui ne commence qu'après dix heures du soir. Épuisés, nous nous asseyons sur le bord encerclant la pyramide de verre et à cet instant une lumière nous éblouit du fond de la coupole. Un bref instant, nous sommes aveuglés, mais quand la clarté s'empare de nouveau de nos yeux, nous apercevons une jeune japonaise tout à fait au fond de ce puits asséché. Et il nous semble qu'elle nous fait des signes. Elle exulte de joie: elle vient de nous confiner sur sa photographie.

— *Miroslav Kirin*
(traduit par Brankica Radić)

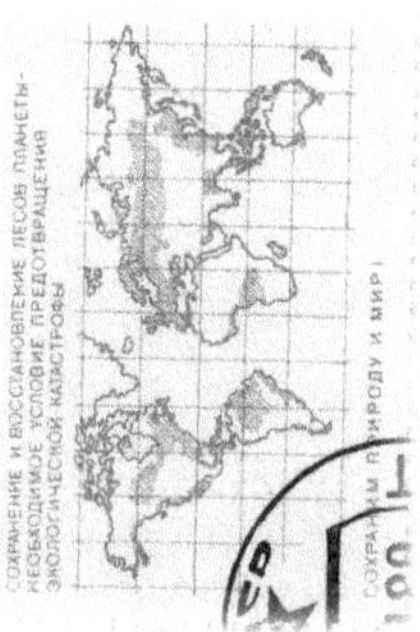

miLogo núm. 42

En una película japonesa clásica, un pozo de agua en la cima de una colina esconde a una víctima de una pelea de amantes. Está lejos de los ojos curiosos, lejos del mundo murmurante, pero nunca fuera de alcance y al final los ojos no deseados realmente se presentan a sí y todo que se supuso quedarse escondido y suprimido surge desde del fondo del pozo.

En medio del amplio patio del Museo del Louvre, una cúpula de cristal esconde uno de estos pozos, las cámaras subterráneas del Museo, más bien, alberga una biblioteca y una tienda de turistas. Como si el Museo quiere realmente detener a sus visitantes, tal vez incluso encarcelarlos.

Una blanca noche *Parisienne* se desciende, empezando sólo después de las diez. Exhaustos, nos sentamos en el borde rodeando la cúpula de cristal y al instante nos deslumbra una luz que viene desde el fondo de la cúpula. Por un momento nos priva de la vista, pero cuando nuestros ojos se recuperan del flash, vemos a una joven japonesa en el fondo de ese pozo seco. Y parece que nos está saludando. Ella está eufuva: acaba de encarcelarnos en una fotografía.

— *Miroslav Kirin*
(traducción, T. Warburton y Bajo y rvb)

Jalog br. 60

iz usta mi ispada jezik
to više nije jezik to je golema jetra teleća
          onog teleta što su ga zaklali prekjučer
uvjerava me mesar moje omiljene mesnice
          ali ja u mesnicu niti nisam otišao
nemam ni omiljenu mesnicu
samo mi je jezik ispao iz usta
          ta golema jetra
vraćam je u usta guram u grlo
odustajem kad shvatim da me guši
moj jezik ponovno ispada
vješa se plazi po vratu liže tijelo
moj jezik moj jezik moj preveliki jezik

— *Miroslav Kirin*

iLogue No. 60

my tongue is falling out of my mouth
it's not even a tongue anymore, it's a huge veal liver
        from the veal they slaughtered two days ago
or so the butcher from my favourite butcher's
wants me to believe
        but I never went to the butcher's
nor do I have a favourite butcher's
my tongue simply fell out of my mouth
        a huge liver
and I push it back into my mouth, I stuff it down my throat
and I give up when I realise it suffocates me
my tongue falls out again
hanging, slithering, down my neck, licking my body
my tongue, my tongue, my most grievous tongue

— *Miroslav Kirin*
(translated fr. the Croatian, Ana Katana)

Nulogue n°60

la langue me tombe de la bouche
ce n'est plus une langue c'est le foie de veau immense
        de ce veau égorgé avant-hier
m'assure le boucher de ma boucherie préférée
        mais je ne suis même pas allé à la boucherie
je n'ai même pas de boucherie préférée
c'est juste ma langue qui m'est tombée de la bouche
        ce foie immense
je le rentre dans la bouche le pousse dans la gorge
je renonce quand je réalise qu'il m'étrangle
ma langue tombe à nouveau
pendouille rampe sur le cou lèche le corps
ma langue ma langue c'est ma trop grande langue

— *Miroslav Kirin*
(traduit par Martina Kramer)

manoLogas nr. 60

Mano liežuvis iškrenta man iš burnos,
tačiau tai jau nebe liežuvis, o didžiulio veršiuko kepenys,
veršiuko, kurį mes vakar papjovėm,
patikino mane mano mėgstamiausios mėsinės mėsininkas.
Tačiau nėjau į jokią mėsinę,
ir apskritai neturiu mėgstamiausios mėsinės.
Tai mano liežuvis, šios didžiulės kepenys,
iškrito man iš burnos,
dedu į burną ir stumiu atgal į gerklę,
pasiduodu, kai suprantu, kad jis mane dusina.
Mano liežuvis vėl iškrenta,
prikimba prie manęs, šliaužia kaklu ir laižo mano kūną.
Per liežuvį, per mano liežuvį, per mano vargana liežuvį.

— *Miroslav Kirin*
(Vertė Džiugas Stanevičius)

miLoga num. 60

Mi lengua cae de mi boca
es no más una lengua es un enorme hígado del
    ternero que hemos sacrificado el día antes de ayer
el carnicero de mi carnicería favorita me asegura
    pero no fui a la carnicería
y tampoco tengo una carnicero favorito
es mi lengua que ha caído de mi boca
    este hígado enorme
lo estoy regresando de nuevo empujándolo en mi garganta
me doy por vencido cuando me doy cuenta de que me está ahog-
    ando
mi lengua cae otra vez
y cuelga sobre mí, sube sigilosamente por mi cuello, lame mi cuerpo
por mi lengua por mi lengua por mi más dolorosa lengua

— *Miroslav Kirin*
(traducción, T. Warburton y Bajo y rvb)

www.ingramcontent.com/pod-product-compliance
Ingram Content Group UK Ltd.
Pitfield, Milton Keynes, MK11 3LW, UK
UKHW020423250726
13967UKWH00007B/2794

9 781684 544707

Gobshite Quarterly

Double Trouble / Issue 36 – Spring 2020

12.00 USDOL | | € 8.03462 EURO | | £ 6.36 GBP (UK) | | $ 12.0281 AUD (Oz) | | $11.4795 CAN | | ¥ 1,179.53 JPY (japan yen) | | 115.380 SAR (S. Africa)

This issue is dedicated to the memory of:

Les Murray (17 Oct., 1938 — 29 Apr., 2019)
Sylvia Miles (9 Sept., 1924 — 12 June, 2019)
Kevin Killian (24 Dec., 1952 — 15 June, 2019)
[Lady] Brenda Maddox [FRSL] (24 Feb., 1932 — 16 June, 2019)
Irene Coates (née Gregory) (23 Mar., 1925 — 18 June 2019)
Geraldine Millais Harcourt (25 May, 1952 — 21 June, 2019)
Édith Scob (21 Oct., 1937 — 26 June 2019)
Ennio Guarnieri (12 Oct., 1930 — 1 July, 2019)
Freddie Jones (12 Sept., 1927 — 9 July, 2019)
Rip Torn (6 Feb., 1931 — 9 July, 2019)
Isaac Lesiba Maphotho (26 Feb., 1931 — 13 July, 2019)
Naomi Ishida 石田 奈央美 (6 Aug., 1969 — 18 July, 2019)
Yoshiji Kigami 木上 益治 (28 Dec., 1957 — 18 July, 2019)
Futoshi Nishiya 西屋 太志 (1981 — 18 July, 2019)
Yasuhiro Takemoto (武本 康弘 (5 Apr., 1972 — 18 July, 2019)
Rutger Hauer (23 Jan., 1944 — 19 July, 2019)
Art Neville (17 Dec., 1937 — 22 July, 2019)
Hal Prince (30 Jan., 1928 — 31 July, 2019)
D.A. Pennebaker (15 July, 1925 — 1 Aug., 2019)
Toni Morrison (18 Feb., 1931 — 5 Aug., 2019)
Larry Siegel (29 Oct., 1925 — 20 Aug., 2019)
Elaine Feinstein (24 Oct., 1930 – 23 Sept., 2019)
Jacques Chirac (29 Nov., 1932 — 26 Sept., 2019)
Gennadi Manakov Геннадий Манаков (1 June, 1950 — 26 Sept., 2019)
Joseph Charles Wilson (6 Nov., 1949 — 27 Sept., 2019)
José José (17 Feb., 1948 — 28 Sept., 2019)
Jessye Norman (15 Sept., 1945 — 30 Sept., 2019)
Ginger Baker (19 Aug., 1939 — 6 Oct., 2019)
Giya Kancheli (Georgian: გია ყანჩელი) (10 Aug., 1935 — 2 Oct., 2019)
Ciaran Carson (9 Oct., 1948 — 6 Oct., 2019)
Robert Forster (13 July, 1941 — 11 Oct., 2019)

Double Trouble / Issue 35 – Winter 2020

Gobshite Quarterly

12.00 USDOL | | € 8.03462 EURO | | £ 6.36 GBP (UK) | | $ 12.0281 AUD (Oz) | | $11.4795 CAN | | ¥ 1,179.53 JPY (japan yen) | | 115.380 SAR (S. Africa)

Gobshite Quarterly
Double Trouble / Issue 32 – Spring 2020

Miroslav Kirin in live performance, 24 May, 2019, Zagreb, Croatia.

You, with your hair swinging left-right / Ti koja kosom mlataraš lijevo-desno. / Tú con tu pelo balanceándose a izquierda-derecha

The Usual Suspects
STAFF

Editor R. V. BRANHAM

Co-editor M.F. MCAULIFFE

Office Mgr. SOFIA SENSEI SATORI ŠOSTAKOVNA SATYAGRAHA STOLIČNIYA SASHIMI SHITKICKER

Assoc. Editor T. WARBURTON Y BAJO

Contrib. Editors T. WARBURTON Y BAJO & CHANNING DODSON & MICHAEL LOHR & DOUGLAS SPANGLE

Field Correspondent MICHAEL LOHR

House Tr. T. WARBURTON Y BAJO (SP.), MIGUEL CAMINHÃO (PORTUGUESE), チャニング・ドッドソン (JAPANESE). Алекса Сигала & Андрей Сен-Сеньков (RUSSIAN), ANI GJIKA (ALBANIAN), ANGGO GENORGA (TAGALOG), MICHAEL LOHR (SCAND.) & RVB (SP., & SELECT ENG.), & ANA KATANA & DIJANA JACOVAK (CROATIAN) & A COHORT OF LITHUANIAN TRANSLATORS

House Spanish Copyediting LYDA ALVAREZ, M.F. MCAULIFFE

Cover Illo GRAHAM K. WILLOUGHBY *Design* T. WARBURTON Y BAJO

Cover comix & phfoto illos & franking VAR. POSTAL SERVICES

Photos (except as noted) M. F. MCAULIFFE, T. WARBURTON Y BAJO

Layout T. WARBURTON Y BAJO & R. V. BRANHAM

Prod. Tools INDESIGN, PHOTOSHOP (OCCASIONALLY, WHEN FUNCTIONAL), GIMP, DREAMSCOPE

Tech Support SAM WARD

Additional Editorial & Design Assistance DOUGLAS SPANGLE & M.F. MCAULIFFE

Legal PETER SHAVER/SOUND ADVICE LLC

Publisher GOBQ LLC/REPROBATE BOOKS

DOUBLE TROUBLE FLIPBOOK DOUBLE ISSUES PRINTED NOV. & MAY OF EA. YEAR.

Post-production printing INGRAM SPARK/LIGHTNING SOURCE

Also distrib. & printed nationally & internationally through INGRAM SPARK/LIGHTNING SOURCE POD

SOLD THROUGH INDEPENDENT BOOKSTORES & AVAILABLE THROUGH INGRAM & AMAZON DOT COM & GOBSHITEQUARTERLY DOT COM

P.R. P. H. VAZAK

Gobshite Quarterly: Double Trouble, Nos. 35/36, Winter & Spring 2020

$12.00 US

ISBN 978-1-68454-470-7

GobQ volunteers: Qualified candidates please send résumé to

GobQ LLC, 338 NE Roth St., Portland, OR 97211, or to gobq at yahoo dot com

Respectfully flip the book over, as Issue 35, Winter 2020, is a whole upsy-daisy 78 pgs away fr. the Spring 2020 issue

Gob Words A word to give offense, when offense may be due. ***Gobshite***, per OED, is what the American crew of Adm. Perry's Expedition to Japan were called by the natives; Amer. Heritage Dictionary, 4th. ed., refers to a wad of expectorated chaw & to the Old Eng. *Shiten*; yet another dictionary refers to a Gobshite as a "*pernicious blatherskite*"— i.e., teleprompter feed-reading stiff for CNN or Rupert Murdoch's Fox "*News*" bullshit mtn. Those offended by the word can now be offended trilingually & quadrilingually, because all Eng.-lang. pces have foreign lang. *en-face* escorts, whether Spanish, Arabic, Icelandic, Farsi, Albanian, Finnish, French, Portuguese, Italian, Russian, Lithuanian, Gaelic, Japanese, Korean, Bangla, or whatever language puts on its UN Observer cap. Wasn't it Pulitzer who sd. journalism should comfort the afflicted & afflict the comfortable? Finally, a Rosetta Stone for the New World Order. — ***rvb***

The Usual Suspects
Contributors

Ivan Antić did the Serbian tr. of Slovienian writer Andrej Blatnik's feuillitons, *Astral Separation/Astralna ločitev/Astralni razvod,* Most Exciting/Najbolj vznemirljivo/Najuznemirljivije, *We're not/Nisva/Nismo* (feuilliton).

Miglė Anušauskaitė, returns w/her Lithuanian tr. of Michael Fikaris' *useless pulgrim/nenaudingas piligrimas* (comix)(komiksas); & remember, keep watching the skies.

Amy Baskin, based in Little Beirut, OR., is a 2019 Oregon Literary Arts Fellowship recipient whose pomes have been in *Dirty Chai, The Ghazal Page, & Cirque*. She makes her GobQ debut w/ 3 pomes, *Where Is The Cap?, Scintillant, & What I Know Every Time We Get Behind the Wheel.*

Selena Bekakis, holder of three design patents, watercolourist, who can be found naked on Netflicks, & who claims to have left her heart in Santorini, twice, makes her *GobQ* debut w/ a poetic collab. w/ Natashia Minto, *Air*.

Jérôme Bihan provided the French texts for Oz cartoonist Michael Fikaris' *useless pulgrim/futile pèlerin*, org. published as part of a series by in France by *Radio As Paper* (comix)(comic)(comíc).

Tomislav Marijan Bilosnić, a Croatian poet who lives in Zadar, returns w/*Balanski Blues/Balkan Blues* (pjesma) (pome).

Andrej Blatnik, who lives in Slovenia, returns w/ a few feuillitons: *Astralna ločitev/Astral Separation, Najbolj vznemirljivo/Most Exciting, & Nisva/We're Not.*

Justina Deksnytė did the Lithuanian tr. of Croatian poet Evilina Rudan's *The Bridge/Most/Tiltas* (pome)(pjesma) (poema).

Hana Dada Banak did the Eng. tr. of Croatian poet Evilina Rudan's *The Bridge/Most* (pome)(pjesma).

Лидија Димковка provided the Macedonian tr. of Slovenian Andre Blatnik's *Astralna ločitev/Астрална разделба/Astral Separation, Najbolj vznemirljivo/Most Exciting/Највознемирувачкото, & Nisva/Не сме/We're Not* (feuilliton).

Marjeta Drobnič provided the Spanish tr. of Slovenian Andre Blatnik's *Astralna ločitev/Separación astral/Astral Separation, Najbolj vznemirljivo/Lo más inquietante/Most Exciting, & Nisva/No Somos/We're Not* (feuilliton).

Kurt Eisenlohr, our metaphysically obstinate semiotic ghost, returns to *GobQ* w/ 3 more reconstructions/deconstructions from his extensive portfolio.

Marcos Farrajota provided Portuguese texts for Oz cartoonist Michael Fikaris' *useless pulgrim/peregrino inútil*, org. part of a series in France published by *Radio As Paper*. (comix)(comíc).

Ann Farley, caregiver & poet who lives in Beaverton, is happiest outside, preferably at the beach. Ann's pomes have been published in *Voicecatcher, RAIN, Third Wednesday, The Avocet*. She makes her GobQ debut w/ two pomes, *Dahlias, & Window*. Expect to see more in future issues.

Michael Fikaris, Melbourne, Vic.-based cartoonist, illustrator & freq. GobQ contrib. returns w/2 pces., *end points/puntos finales/krajnja tocke/lokapunktar*, made for the *hold on* exhib., rubicon art, melb., vic., oz., 7—24 nov., 2018 , & *useless pulgrim* (presented in its en-face parallel-texted glory), & orig. published as part of a series in France by *Radio As Paper*. (comix)(comíc).

Roman Karlović, provided the English tr. of Croatian poet Tomislav Marijan Bilosnić's *Balanski Blues/Balkan Blues* (pjesma)(pome).

Ana Katana returns to *GobQ* w/ her Croat. tr. tr. of Spanish essayist Aarón Rodríguez' *4 preguntas y 4 hipótesis para pensar Blade Runner 2049 de Denis Villenueve/4 pitanja i 4 hipoteze za razmišljanje o filmu Blade Runner 2049 Denisa Villeneuvea/4 Questions & 4 Hypotheses for Pondering Denis Villeneuve's Blade Runner 2049* (ensayo) (esej)(essay).

Christoph Keller, now residing in St. Galen, Switz., returns w/ *A Les Murray Memoir*, about his friendship w/ the Oz poet.

Michael Lohr returns w/ his Icelandic tr. of Amy Baskin's *Where Is the Cap?/Hvar er Húfa?, What I know Every Time We Get Behind the Wheel/Hvað eg veit hverju tið við fyrir hjálið, Scintillant/Ljóma* (pome)(ljóð), Christoph Keller's *A Les Murray Memoir/Ævisaga* (memoir)(ævisaga), of Spanish essayist Aarón Rodríguez' 4 *preguntas y 4 hipó-*

tesis para pensar Blade Runner 2049 de Denis Villenueve/ Fjórir spurningar og fjórar tilgátur til að hugleiða Blade Runner 2049 is Denis Villeneuve/ 4 Hypotheses for Pondering Denis Villeneuve's Blade Runner 2049 (ensayo)(ritgerð) (essay), & the Nastashia Minto & Selena Bekakis collab., *Air/Loft* (pome)(ljóð).

Nastashia Minto, Georgia-born & Little Beirut-based, is the author the acclaimed memoir, *Naked*, from Eldredge Books. Her writing, which explores intersectionalities of family, faith, race, sexuality, love, abuse, & identity, has appeared in *SUSAN* & the third *Unchaste Anthol*. Natashia makes her *GobQ* debut w/ a poetic collab. w/ Selena Bekakis, *Air*.

Dominykas Norkūnas returns w/ a Lithuanian tr. of the Nastashia Minto & Selena Bekakis collab., *Air/Oras* (pome)(poema).

Jelena Pataki returns w. Croatian tr. of Christoph Keller's *A Les Murray Memoir/Memoar o Murrayju* (memoir)(memoar), as well as the poetic collab. of Nastashia Minto & Salena Bekakis, *Air/Zrak* (pome) (pjesma), & Spanish essayist Aarón Rodríguez' *4 preguntas y 4 hipótesis para pensar Blade Runner 2049 de Denis Villenueve/4 Questions & 4 Hypotheses for Pondering Denis Villeneuve's Blade Runner 2049* (ensayo)(esej)(essay)(ritgerð).

Jagna Pogačnik did the Croat. tr. of Slovenian writer Andrej Blatnik's feuillitons, *Astralna ločitev/Najuznemirljivije/Astralna rastava/Astral Separation, Najbolj vznemirljivo/Most Exciting, & Nisva/Nismo/We're Not.*

Aarón Rodríguez, who writes for Barcelona's *Transit: cine y otros desviós*, returns w/ *4 preguntas y 4 hipótesis para pensar Blade Runner 2049 de Denis Villenueve/4 Questions & 4 Hypotheses for Pondering Denis Villeneuve's Blade Runner 2049* (ensayo)(essay).

Evelina Rudan, a freq. *GobQ* contrib. & poet based in Zagreb, & tr. living in Moscow, returns w/ Most/The Bridge (pjesma)(pome).

Tamara M. Soban did the English tr. of Slovenia writer Andrej Blatnik's few feuillitons: *Astralna ločitev/Astral Separation, Najbolj vznemirljivo/Most Exciting, & Nisva/ We're Not.*

Florian Vetsch, a Swiss poet & tr. returns w/ a tr. of Christoph Keller's *A Les Murray Memoir/Les Traf Ich 1999* (memoir)(Memoiren).

T. Warburton y Bajo y rvb did co-tr. of a baker's doz. of this issue's works into Spanish, w/ the exception of the Blatnik feuillitons.

Graham Willoughby, whose artwork has adorned our covers since is. no. 2, returns, & still in watery colour! Graham has exhibited in galleries in the US, Germany & his native Oz, & has artist books in museum colls. worldwide.

Lou Reed concert, Greek Theatre, day of the Rodney King verdict; the resulting riots, which I saw some of in my rearview mirror as I made my way to the concert, came to be known by native smart-arses as the United Colours of Benetton Riots. I saw at least 90 bldgs aflame as I drove home on the var. fwys& didn't hear a single siren. That evening, the police chief, at a Republicaño fundraiser, declared that the fires would be allowed to burn a while so that the public would beg the police for law & order. That fall Pappy Bush lost to Clinton. — rvb

Dahlias

I don't want to arrive too early
for the meeting at the rehab center,
so I go to my garden,
cut all the dahlias I have. Four.
They flop around my Goodwill vase.

I cut lemon balm, rose campion, lavender
and two red hot pokers, enough to fill.
Jan is terminal. Rehab seems beside the point.
I've been a caregiver for years,
so the family asked me to come, to talk.
I bring absurdly happy pink dahlias
with yellow centers.
You can't go to a place like that empty handed.

Jan reaches, but hasn't the strength
to hold the vase. We go to a conference room,
place the dahlias on the table.
Jan's daughter moves them aside.

I ask, *What would you like to know?*
I'm no adviser.
I'm there to say what needs to be said:
facility, home, agency, bed bath, morphine,
bed sores, palliative care, hospice.

The daughter asks, *Mom,*
what do you want?

Jan says, *Comfort.*
She gazes at the vase.

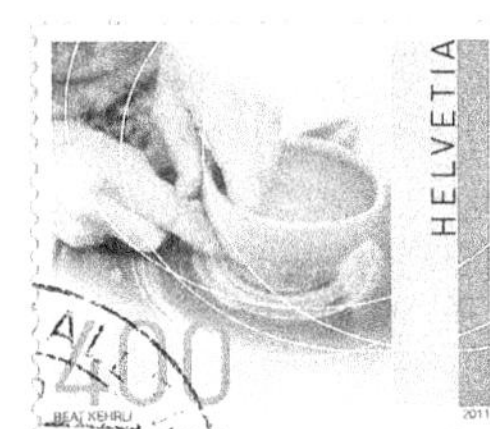

Comfort. No pain.
She is beyond sentences.

Ice cream, she says.
Dahlias.

— *Ann Farley*

July 22, 2019

Dalije

Ne želim stići prerano
na sastanak u centru za odvikavanje,
stoga odlazim u svoj vrt,
režem sve dalije koje imam. Četiri.
Plutaju uokolo u mojoj vazi koju nosim.

Siječem matičnjak, rumenku, lavandu
i dvije tritome, da je popunim.
Jan je neizlječiva. Odvikavanje djeluje besmisleno.
Njegujem je godinama,
stoga me obitelj zamolila da dođem, i razgovaram.
Nosim smiješno vesele ružičaste dalije
sa žutim srcima.
Ne možete na takvo mjesto praznih ruku.

Jan pruža ruku, ali nema snage
držati vazu. Odlazimo u sobu za sastanke,
stavljam daliju na stol,
Janina kći sklanja ih u stranu.

Pitam: *Što vas zanima?*
Nisam savjetnica.
Došla sam reći što treba:
ustanova, kuća, agencija, kupke u krevetu, morfij,
rane od ležanja, palijativna skrb, hospicij.

Kći pita: *Mama,*
što želiš?

Jan kaže: *Udobnost.*
Zuri u vazu.

Udobnost. Bez bola.
Više ne može izgovarati rečenice.

Sladoled, kaže.
Dalije.

— *Ann Farley* — *22. srpnja 2019*
(prijevod, Jelena Pataki)

Dahlias

No quiero llegar demasiado temprano
para la reunión en el centro de rehabilitación,
así que voy a mi jardín,
corto todas las dalias que tengo. Cuatro.
Se arrojan alrededor de mi jarrón de *Goodwill*.

Corto el bálsamo de limón, el almizó, la lavanda y
dos póqueres al rojo vivo, suficientes para llenarlo.
Jan está terminal. La rehabilitación parece inútil.
He sido un cuidador durante años,
así que la familia pidió que yo viniera, hablara.
Traigo dalias felices y absurdamente rosas
con centros amarillos.
No se puede ir a un lugar así con las manos vacías.

Jan alcanza, pero no tiene la fuerza
para sostener el jarrón. Vamos a una sala de conferencias,
ponemos las dalias en la mesa.
La hija de Jan las mueve a un lado.

Pregunto, *¿qué le gustaría saber?*
No soy consejero.
Estoy allí para decir lo que debe decirse:
instalación, a casa, agencia, *Bed Bath* y morfina,
llagas de la cama, cuidados paliativos, hospicio.

La hija pregunta, *mamá,*
¿Qué quieres?

Jan dice, *Comodidad.*
Mira fijamente al jarrón.

Comodidad. Sin dolor.
Está más allá de oraciones.

helado, ella dice.
Dalias.

— *Ann Farley*
(Traducción, T. Warburton y Bajo y rvb)

Window

Move the woman with dementia to a window.
Ask her what she sees.
Go with her.
Tell her *Yes*.

— *Ann Farley*

Little Beirut, Oregon

Prozor

Premjestite dementnu ženu pokraj prozora.
Pitajte je što vidi.
Pođite s njom.
Recite joj *Da*.

— *Ann Farley*
(prijevod, Jelena Pataki — 22. srpnja 2019)

Ventana

Mueva la mujer con demencia a una ventana.
Pregúntale qué ve.
Vaya con ella.
Dígale que *sí*.

— *Ann Farley*
(Traducción, T. Warburton y Bajo y rob)

most

nestašni postolari, ljepljivi prsti, sjajne djevojke
i nešto tastature dostajat će za priču mog života
koju počinjem pisati sada dok vani pršti snijeg
dok prekoputa naša susjeda suši kosu
dok iznutra moj mladić prži krumpir
dok su mi usta suha, a prsti pokretljivi
u toj priči ja nisam sjajna djevojka
ni tajna ljubav neke od sjajnih djevojaka,

nisam nestašni postolar
niti išta ljepljivog ima na meni
mislim da bih mogla biti riba, pas ili mačka
u kući postolareve žene
i da bih je mogla tješiti
kad se bude naginjala kroz prozor
kad bude sanjala dotičuće grane
i kad bude vikala bijesno i uzaludno
mislim da bih mogla biti čavao, koža ili mast
na postolarevu stolu kad bude plakao
ili junački pocupkivao (ako sam mast tad ću se čuvat,
a ako sam čavao čuvat će se oni)
još bih mogla biti sat, torba ili jastuk
mladih, sjajnih djevojaka
što raspršeno kroče mostom
ili taj most sam
kako se uleknjuje i lomi, raspada
pršti kamenje krupno i sitno na sve strane
baš kao i ovaj snijeg vani
dok se prži krumpir
dok se suši kosa
i piše priča

— *Evelina Rudan*

the bridge

lively shoemakers, sticky fingers, remarkable girls
and a keyboard will be sufficient to tell the story of my life-
story I'm starting to write now that snowflakes are pirouetting outside
and our neighbour is drying her hair in the vis-à-vis apartment
my boyfriend is making French fries
and now that my mouth is dry, fingers responsive

I'm not one of the remarkable girls in that story
neither am I one of the remarkable girls' sweethearts
nor am I a lively shoemaker
and there's nothing sticky about me
but I could easily be a fish, a dog or a cat
from the house of the shoemaker's wife
and I could comfort her
when she leans through the window
dreams of adjoining branches
and shouts furiously to no avail
I think I could be a shoe-nail, leather or grease
resting on the shoemaker's desk while he's shedding tears
or skipping in triumph (should it turn out I am to be grease, I will be
wary,
but if I am a shoe-nail, they will have to look out for themselves)
I could also be a watch, a bag or a pillow
belonging to those young, remarkable girls
crossing the bridge ramblingly
or I could be the bridge itself
sagging and breaking, falling apart
stones and rocks sputtering all around
just like the snowflakes outside
potatoes still frying
hair drying
and the story being written

— *Evelina Rudan*
(tr. fr. the Croatian, Hana Dada Banak)

el puente

animados zapateros, dedos pegajosos, chicas notables
y un teclado serán suficientes para contar mi historia-de-vida—
historia que comienzo a escribir ahora que los copos de nieve piruetean
afuera
y nuestra vecina seca su cabello en el piso vis-à-vis
mi novio hace patatas fritas
y ahora que mi boca está seca, los dedos sensibles

No soy una de las chicas notables en esa historia
tampoco soy uno de los amores de las chicas notables
ni soy un zapatero animado
y no hay nada pegajoso acerca de mí
pero podría fácilmente ser un pez, un perro o un gato
en la casa de la esposa del zapatero
y la podría consolar
cuando ella se inclina por la ventana
sueña con ramas contiguas
y grita furiosamente sin resultados
Creo que podría ser un clavo de zapato, cuero o grasa
descansando en el escritorio del zapatero mientras él está derramando
lágrimas
o saltando de triunfo (si resulta que voy a ser grasa, seré cautelosa,
pero si soy clavo de zapato, se tendrán que cuidar)
podría ser también un reloj, una bolsa o una almohada
perteneciendo a esas jóvenes, chicas notables cruzando el puente, diva-
gando
o podría ser el puente en sí
colgando y quebrando, cayendo en pedazos
piedras y rocas salpicando todo alrededor
al igual que los copos de nieve afuera patatas aún friendose
cabello secandose
y la historia escribiendose

— Evelina Rudan
(traducción, T. Warburton y Bajo y rvb)

tiltas

linksmi batsiuviai, lipnūs pirštai, nuostabios merginos
ir klaviatūra yra visa ko užteks papasakoti mano gyvenimo istorijai
kurią aš pradedu rašyti dabar kai lauke krinta sniegas
kai už sienos kaimynė džiovinasi plaukus
kai viduje mano vaikinas kepa bulves
kai mano burna išdžiuvusi, o pirštai juda
toje istorijoje aš nesu nuostabi mergina
nei slapta meilė vienos tų nuostabių merginų,
nesu linkmas batsiuvys
nėra nieko lipnaus apie mane
manau galėčiau būti žuvimi, šunimi ar katinubatsiuvio žmonos
namuose
ir galėčiau ją guosti
kuomet ji pasilenkia pro langą
kuomet ji svajoja paliesti šakas
ir kuomet ji šaukia piktai ir veltui
manau galėčiau būti vinimi, oda ar tepalu
ant batsiuvio stalo kuomet jis verkia
ar šokinėja iš džiaugsmo (jei būčiau tepalu būčiau budrus,
o jei būčiau vinimi jiems teks pasirūpinti savimi)
aš galėčiau būti ir laikrodis, krepšys ar pagalvė
jaunų, nuostabių merginų
kurios vaikštinėja tiltu
arba būčiau pats tiltas
kuris linksta ir byra, trūkinėja
dideli ir maži akmenys krenta aplink
visai kaip lauke sniegas
kaip bulvės kepa
kaip plaukai džiūva
ir istorija rašoma

— *Evelina Rudan*
(vertė Justina Deksnytė)

A Murray Memoir: I met Les in 1999 in Frauenfeld, Switzerland, when he was reading at a poetry festival.

Here he was, the most dignified, compassionate, sharpest and funniest poet of the other (but shouldn't all poets be poets of the other?)—the most human of them all—the sayer of what's right in this unjust world where you get sacked for being different (or, more likely, not hired to begin with)—who had just written the novel-in-verse *Fredy Neptune* about a twentieth-century working-class-hero Ulysses.

Shocked into dis-

LES TRAF ICH 1999 in der Schweiz, in Frauenfeld, wo er an einem Lyrikfestival auftrat. Da war er: der würdevollste, passionierteste, schärfste und witzigste Dichter des Fremden (doch sollten nicht alle Dichter Dichter des Fremden sein?) – der menschlichste unter ihnen allen – der ausspricht, was Recht ist in dieser ungerechten Welt, wo du gefeuert wirst, wenn du von der Norm abweichst (oder, wahrscheinlicher, nicht einmal angestellt) – Les hatte gerade den Versroman *Fredy Neptune* geschrieben, über einen Helden der Arbeiterklasse, einen wahren Odysseus. Dieser Anblick schockt ihn in eine Behinderung: von Kerosin übergos-

Ævisaga: Ég hitti Les árið 1999 í Frauenfeld, Sviss, þegar hann var að lesa á ljóðhátíð. Hér var hann mest dignified, samúðarmaður, skörpasti og skemmtilegasta skáld hins (en ætti ekki allir skáldar að vera skáld hins?) - Maðurinn af þeim öllum, sem segir frá því sem er rétt í þessari óréttlátu heimi þar sem þú fá rekinn til að vera öðruvísi (eða líklega ekki ráðinn til að byrja með) - hver hafði bara skrifað frönsku *Fredy Neptune* í fréttum um tuttugustu aldar verkalýðshreyfinguna Ulysses. Hneykslaður í fötlun með því að sjá skautlausa, fíngerðu, líflegir, armenska

Memoar o Murrayju: Upoznao sam Lesa 1999. u Frauenfeldu u Švicarskoj, gdje je čitao na festivalu poezije. Bio je najdostojanstveniji, najsuosjećajniji, najbistriji i najzabavniji pjesnik drugoga (ali zar svi pjesnici ne bi trebali pjesnici drugoga?) – najveći čovjek od svih njih – govorio je što je ispravno na ovome neprevedenom svijetu gdje vas najure zato što ste drugačiji (odnosno, još vjerojatnije, uopće ne dobijete posao) – koji je upravo napisao roman u stihovima *Fredy Neptune* o dvadesetostoljetnom junaku radničke klase Uliksu. Šokiran do nemoći

Una Memoria de Les Murray: Conocí a Les en 1999 en Frauenfeld, Suiza, cuando leía en un festival de la poesía.

Aquí estaba, el más digno, compasivo, más agudo y más gracioso poeta del otro (pero no deberían todos los poetas ser poetas del otro?) — el más humano de todos ellos — el que dice lo que está bien en este mundo injusto en el que te despiden por ser diferente (o, más probable, no contratado para empezar) — que acababa de escribir la novela en el verso Fredy Neptune sobre trabajadora de clase obrera-héroe Ulises del siglo XX.

Sorprendido por la discapacidad por la vista de mujeres armenias empapadas de queroséno,

ability by the sight of kerosene-drenched, set-afire-alive Armenian women forced into dancing by laughing Turks (*"These eyes of mine— / How shall I dig the eyes out, how shall I, how?"* from Siamanto's epigraph to *Fredy Neptune*), Fredy develops superpowers that are questionable as superpowers are: he stops feeling pain (his *"numb talent"*) and develops superhuman strength, bending iron and lifting freight cars. So there I was, drinking a glass of milk with Fredy's creator; (Les later denied that was all he was drinking). Then, just as weight-defying as his creation, he carried me on his back up the heavy stairs to where he was giving his reading.

And what a reading he gave, impersonating his poems, a little breathless, I thought,

sene, bei lebendigem Leib angezündete armenische Frauen, welche die Türken lachend zu tanzen zwangen (*"Diese meine Augen – / Wie soll ich sie aus ihren Höhlen reissen, wie nur, wie?"* aus Siamantos Epigraph auf *Fredy Neptune*), Fredy entwickelt Superkräfte, die wie alle Superkräfte hinterfragbar sind: Er hört auf, Schmerz zu empfinden (sein *"taubes Talent"*), und setzt übermenschliche Kräfte frei, biegt Eisenstangen und stemmt Güterwaggons. Und nun sass ich mit dem Schöpfer von Fredy da und trank ein Glas Milch mit ihm (Les bestritt später, dass das alles sei, was er trinke). Dann trug er, selber so kräftig wie seine Kreatur, mich auf seinem Rücken die steilen Stufen zur Bühne hoch, auf der er seine Lesung geben würde. Und was für eine Lesung er gab, er verkörperte seine Gedichte voll und ganz, ein wenig ausser Atem, ich vermutete wegen mir, weil er mich eben erst

konur þvinguðust í dans með því að hlæja Turks (*"Þessi augu mín / / Hvernig skal ég grafa augun út, hvernig skal ég, hvernig?"* Frá Epigraph Siamanto til Fredy Neptune), Fredy þróar stórveldi sem eru vafasöm þar sem stórveldir eru: hann hættir að finna fyrir sársauka (*"dofinn hæfileikar"* hans) og þróar ofhuman styrk, beygja járn og lyfta vöruflutningum. Svo þarna var ég að drekka glas af mjólk með skapara Fredy Neptune. (Les neitaði síðar að það væri allt sem hann var að drekka). Þá, rétt eins og þyngd-defying eins og sköpun hans, flutti hann mig á bakinu hans upp í mikla stigann þar sem hann var að lesa hann. Og hvaða lesa hann gaf, lék ljóð sín, smá anda, hugsaði ég, vegna þess að ég hafði bara borið mig upp flug af slökkvistarfi. Síðan, þegar hann er

prizorom Armenki polivenih kerozinom i živih zapaljenih od strane nasmijanih Turaka (*„Te moje oči – / Kako ću ih iskopati, kako ću, kako?“* iz Siamantova epigrafa, *Fredy Neptune*), Fredy razvije supermoći, upitne kako to supermoći obično bivaju: prestaje osjećati bol (njegov *„tupi talent“*) i razvija nadljudsku snagu, savija željezo i podiže teretne vagone. I tako sam pio mlijeko s Fredyjevim tvorcem (Les je poslije zanijekao da je pio samo to). Zatim me, baš poput njegova stvorenja otpornog na teret, na leđima odnio teškim stubama do mjesta na kojem je čitao. I to kako je čitao, utjelovljujući svoje pjesme, pomalo zadihan, pomislio sam, zbog mene, jer me nosio zahtjevnim stubištem. Otada, kad je u New Yorku, zajedno jedemo krezle (on je, ja sam jeo

prendidas en llamas, forzadas a bailar por los turcos riendo (*“estos ojos míos—¿cómo voy a cavar los ojos, ¿cómo voy a, cómo?”* desde el epígrafo de Siamanto a Fredy Neptune), Fredy desarrolla superpotencias que son cuestionables como superpotencias son: deja de sentir dolor (su *“talento insensible”*) y desarrolla fuerza sobrehumana, doblando hierro y levantando carros de carga. Así que allí estaba, bebiendo un vaso de leche con el creador de Fredy; (Les negó más tarde que era todo lo que estaba bebiendo). Entonces, igual que desafiando el peso como su creación, me llevó en su espalda por las pesadas escaleras hasta donde daba su lectura.

Y lo que una lectura que dio, haciéndose pasar por sus poemas, un poco sin aliento, pensé, por mi culpa, después de haberme llevado a un vuelo de escaleras incapacitantes.

Desde entonces, cuando está en Nueva York, comemos pan dulce jun-

because of me, having just carried me up a flight of disabling stairs.

Ever since, when he's in New York, we eat sweetbread together (he did, I had pork chops), go for (very short) city walks, pee in robber baron mansions (he did, I used the bathroom).

Les travels a lot, I not so much anymore.

Les is the bravest of men, with so many ailments, health problems, disabilities that he writes about—just for me, I imagine, when I'm reading you, dear faraway friend.

— *Christoph Keller*

die mühsamen Stufen hochgetragen hatte. Seither essen wir immer, wenn er in New York ist, Kalbsbries zusammen (er schon, ich nehme Schweinekoteletts), wir machen (sehr kurze) Stadtspaziergänge, pinkeln in Villen von Raubkapitalisten (er schon, ich benutze die Toilette). Les reist viel, nicht mehr so häufig. Les ist der Tapferste aller Männer, mit so vielen Leiden, Gesundheitsproblemen, Behinderungen, über die er schreibt – nur für mich, stelle ich mir vor, wenn ich dich lese, lieber ferner Freund.

— *Christoph Keller*
(aus dem Amerikanischen von Florian Vetsch)

í New York, borðum við sælgæti saman (hann gerði, ég hafði svínakjöt), farið í (mjög stuttar) borgarferðir, kýpur í ránbarrihúsum (hann gerði, ég notaði baðherbergið). Les ferðast mikið, ég er ekki svo mikið lengur. Les er djörfungur karla, með svo margar lasleiki, heilsufarsvandamál, fötlun sem hann skrifar um - bara fyrir mig, ímynda mér, þegar ég er að lesa þig, góða farinn vinur.

— *Christoph Keller*
(Þýtt úr Ensku, Michael Lohr)

svinjske kotlete, odlazimo na (vrlo kratke) šetnje gradom, piškimo u palačama baruna razbojnika (on je, ja sam se poslužio zahodom). Les često putuje, ja više ne toliko. Les je najhrabriji među ljudima, s toliko boljki, zdravstvenih problema, poteškoća o kojima piše - samo za mene, zamišljam, dok te čitam, dragi daleki prijatelju.

— Christoph Keller (prijevod, Jelena Pataki)

tos (lo hizo, yo tenía chuletas de cerdo), ir por (muy corto) paseos por la ciudad, mear en mansiones de barón del ladrón (lo hizo, yo usé el baño).

Les viaja mucho, yo no tanto más.

Les es el más valiente de hombres, con tantas dolencias, problemas de salud, discapacidades de que escribe — sólo para mí, imagino, cuando te leo, querido amigo lejano.

— Christoph Keller (Traducción, T. Warburton y Bajo y rvb)

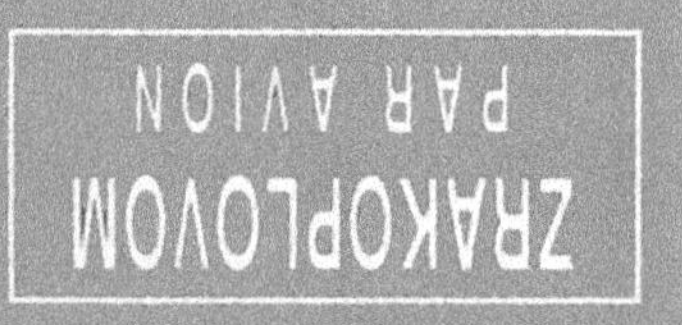

BALKAN BLUES

I don't care about abstractions, biochemistry,
fear and fortune-telling.
I have no idea what I want,
but I know how to get it with a penknife.
My brothers are all poppy pickers, killers,
with such a big heart you could drown in it.
I'm the runner type—always galloping—
but not a horse: I let nobody fuck with me.
I live on lies
and break on clouds.

— *Tomislav Marijan Bilosnić*
(Tr. fr. the Croatian, Roman Karlović)

BALKANSKI BLUES

Ne zanima me apstraktno, biokemija,
strah i proricanje.
Ne znam što hoću,
ali znam kako se to postiže čakijom.
Moja su braća berači maka, ubojice,
imaju dušu u kojoj se možeš utopiti.
Trkači sam tip, u galopu,
a ne dam se zajebavati kao konj.
Od laži živim
i razbijam se među oblacima.

— *Tomislav Marijan Bilosnić*

BLUES BALCÁNICOS

No me importan las abstracciones, la bioquímica,
el miedo y la adivinación.
No tengo ningún idea de lo que quiero,
pero sé cómo conseguirlo con una navaja.
Mis hermanos son todos recolectores de la amapola, asesinos,
con un corazón tan grande que podría ahogarse en el.
Soy del tipo corredor, siempre galopando,
pero no soy caballo: no dejo a nadie joder conmigo.
Vivo de mentiras
y ruptura en las nubes.

— *Tomislav Marijan Bilosnić*
(Traducción, T. Warburton y Bajo y rvb)

Балканский блюз

Меня не волнуют абстракции, биохимия,
страх или предсказания.
Я понятия не имею, чего хочу,
но знаю, как выковырить это перочинным ножом.
Мои братья - сборщики мака и наемные убийцы
с такими огромными сердцами, что ты можешь утонуть в них.
Я бегу - всегда галопом —
но я не лошадь: никому не позволяю трахнуть меня.
Я живу во лжи
и разбиваюсь об облака.

— *Томислав Марийан билосниц*
(Перевод на русский Андрея Сен-Сенькова)

WHERE IS THE CAP?

Pink strips the skin.
Red thins the blood.
Green slows the pulse.
Yellow takes away the pain
and ruptures colons.

Cheaper up north
if you can get them.
Spill the damage.
Break open
the fine print.

Serve with screwtop plastic eggs,
fabricated grass, and
hollow milk bunny chasers.
Call 911!
Rise!

They were meant to grant you
new life, sweetness!
Quick—which color induces
vomit?
What combination pumps
the stomach?

Where is the seal?
The lid?
The cover?
The shroud?
Blue stops the heart.

— *Amy Baskin*

¿DÓNDE ESTÁ LA TAPA?

El color de rosa despoja la piel.
Rojo adelgaza la sangre.
Verde ralentiza el pulso.
Amarillo se quita el dolor
y ruptura los colones.

Más baratos por el norte
si puedes obtenerlos.
Derrama el daño.
Abre
la letra pequeña.

Sirve con huevos de plástico
atornillados,
hierba fabricada y
cazadores de conejos de leche hueca.
¡Llama al 911!
¡Levántate!

Estaban destinados a concederte
nueva vida, ¡dulzura¡
Rápido: ¿qué color induce el vómito?
¿Qué combinación bombea
el estómago?

¿Dónde está el sello?
¿La tapa?
¿La cubierta?
¿El sudario?
Azul parará el corazón.

— *Amy Baskin*
(Traducción, T. Warburton y Bajo y rvb)

GDJE JE ČEP?

Ružičasta guli kožu.
Crvena razrjeđuje krv.
Zelena usporava bilo.
Žuta uklanja bol
i buši slijepo crijevo

Sjeverno su jeftinije
ako ih se uspiješ domoći.
Razlijj štetu
Razbij
sitna slova upute

Posluži uz plastična jaja plutenog
okusa,
umjetnu travu, i
zalij mlijekom.
Zovi 911!
Ustaj!

Trebali su ti podariti novi život!
Slatkoću!
Brzo – koja boja izaziva povraćanje?
Koja kombinacija ispumpava
želudac?

Gdje je pečat?
A poklopac?
A zatvarač?
A mrtvački pokrov?
Plava zaustavlja srce.

— *Amy Baskin*
(Prijevod, Ana Katana)

HVAR ER HÚFA?

Bleikir strimla húðina.
Rauður þynnir blóðið.
Grænt hægir á púlsinum.
Gult tekur frá sársaukanum
og rofnar ristli.

Ódýrari upp fyrir norðan
ef þú getur fengið þau.
Spillið tjónið.
Brotið opið
smáa letrið.

Berið fram með skrúfuðum
plastseggjum,
tilbúið gras, og
holur mjólkur kanínukastarar.
Hringdu í 911!
Rísu upp!

Þeim var ætlað að veita þér
nýtt líf, sætleikur!
Fljótur — hvaða litur vekur
uppköst?
Hvaða samsetning dælur
maginn?
Hvar er selurinn?
Lokið?
Kápan?
Skjólinn?
Blátt stoppar hjartað.

— *Amy Baskin*
(Þýtt úr Ensku, Michael Lohr)

WHAT I KNOW EVERY TIME WE GET BEHIND THE WHEEL

—to my sister, who wasn't as lucky

Stars tunnel, vision to black. Heads don't
even need to hit dashboards, the adverse
ramming his SUV into the passenger side.

Once, heart pulsed in the belly. Now, liquid
spurts from tailpipe, windows, veins, and
eyes.

I am here because two kids drove back
from Pike's Peak with a wine-stained picnic blanket
and high blood-alcohol content.

I was handed my own set of car keys when I
turned sixteen, before I had even changed
out of my pjs.

At some church, a lilac tree is forever planted in
your name. By the Flatirons, we dressed a bench
with a plaque, before you had even graduated.

— Amy Baskin

ŠTO ZNAM SVAKI PUT KAD SJEDNEM ZA UPRAVLJAČ

—mojoj sestri, koja nije imala toliko sreće

Zvijezde se vrtlože, pred očima se mrači. Glave čak
ne udaraju o vjetrobransko staklo, dok
se SUV zabija u suvozača.

Nekoć je srce pulsiralo u utrobi. Sada tekućina
štrca iz ispušne cijevi, kroz prozore, iz vena i
očiju.

Ja sam ovdje jer se dvoje klinaca vozilo
s Pikeovog vrha s mrljama od vina na izletničkoj dekici
i mnogo promila u krvi.

Meni su dali ključeve auta
kad sam navršila šesnaest.
Bila sam još bunovna, u pidžami.

Kraj neke crkve, jorgovan će zauvijek cvjetati
u tvoje ime. Podno Flatirona obilježili smo klupu
plaketom tebi u čast, a nisi još ni maturirala.

— Amy Baskin
(Prijevod, Ana Katana)

LO QUE SÉ CADA VEZ QUE PORERMOS DÉTRAS DEL VOLANTE

— a mi hermana, que no estuvo tan afortunada

Túnel y estrellas, visión a negro. Las cabezas ni
siquiera necesitan golpear los tableros, el adverso
chocar su SUV en el lado del pasajero.

Una vez, el corazón palpitó en el vientre. Ahora, liquido
brota desde el tubo de escape, de ventanas, venas y
ojos.

Estoy aquí porque dos niños regresaron
de Pico de Pike con una manta para picnic manchada por el vino
y alto contenido de alcohol en el sangre.

me entregaron mis propios llaves de coche cuando
cumplí dieciséis, antes de que yo había cambiado
de mis pjs.

En alguna iglesia, un árbol lila se planta para siempre en
tu nombre. Junto a las planchas de hierro, vestimos un banco
con una placa, incluso antes de que te graduaras.

— *Amy Baskin*
(Traducción, T. Warburton y Bajo y rvb)

HVAÐ ÉG VEIT HVERJU TÍÐ VIÐ FYRIR HJÁLIÐ

— Til systur minnar, sem var ekki eins heppin

Stjörnugöng, sýn að svörtu. Hausar ekki
þarf jafnvel að lemja á mælaborð, slæmu
rammar jeppa sínum í farþegahliði-na.

Einu sinni ruddist hjartað í magann. Nú, vökvi
spurts frá rófu, gluggum, æðum og
augu.

Ég er hér vegna þess að tvö börn keyrðu til baka
frá Pike's Peak með vínlitaðri lau-tarferð teppi
og hátt alkóhólinnihald í blóði.

Mér var afhent mitt eigið bíllykla þegar ég
varð sextán, áður en ég hafði jafnvel skipt um
út af pjs mínum.

Í einhverri kirkju er lilac tré plantað að eilífu í
nafn þitt. Við Flatirons klæddum okkur bekk
með veggskjöldur, áður en þú hafðir jafnvel útskrifast.

— *Amy Baskin*
(Þýtt úr Ensku, Michael Lohr)

SCINTILLANT

"Vintage" Edison LED bulbs sear my eyes and brain
to the point where I need medication to function and

sunglasses to navigate my way through the living
world, the living room.

My partner knows me. Knows that I will take months
to decide upon paint chips and upholstery fabric,

knows that I prefer the dark with a smattering of
seasonal lights strung along the mantle with few lumens,

and he thinks he understands why, though it bothers him
that I am not moved by his need for brightness.

He thinks he knows me, but he cannot know me.
He cannot see through my eyes, and though truly

I wish I could, I cannot escape my head and settle
comfortably behind the ridge of his forehead, either.

Current top relationship experts insist we should not know
everything about each other. Leave the candle of mystery lit.

Learn everything and risk dousing all the flames of passion.
Lean in too close and risk smoldering that flame.

I say fine to all this. Let's give our candle plenty of air.
May it burn hot, but — can we cover it with a lampshade?

— *Amy Baskin*

SVJETLUCAVO

Edisonove "vintage" LED žarulje žare mi oči i mozak
toliko da trebam lijekove za svakodnevni život,

sunčane naočale za plovidbu
svijetom živih i dnevnim boravkom.

Moj partner me poznaje. Zna da se mjesecima
premišljam o boji i tapacirungu,

zna da volim tamno s pokojim lumenom
nejakog blagdanskog osvjetljenja nad kaminom,

I misli da razumije zašto je tako, mada mu smeta
što me njegova potreba za svjetlom ne dira.

Misli da me poznaje, ali ne može on to.
Ne može gledati mojim očima i premda bih zaista

htjela da mogu, ja ne mogu izići iz svoje glave
i ušuškati se iza grebena njegova čela.

Današnji stručnjaci za odnose tvrde da ne trebamo znati sve jedni o
drugima. Neka svijeća gori tajanstvenim plamom.

Saznamo li sve, riskiramo gušenje plamenja strasti.
Približimo li se odveć, izgorjet ćemo.

Može, što se mene tiče. Neka se plamen napaja zrakom.
Neka plamti vrelinom, ali – možemo li ga pokriti abažurom?

— *Amy Baskin*
(Prijevod, Ana Katana)

CENTELLEAR

Bombillas "Atiguo" Edison LED queman mis ojos y cerebro
hasta el punto en que necesito medicamentos para funcionar y

gafas de sol para navegar por el mundo
vivo, por la sala festivo.

Mi pareja me conoce. Sabe que tomaré meses
decidir sobre las virutas de pintura y tela de tapicería,

sabe que prefiero la oscuridad con un puñado de
luces con pocos lúmenes estacionales colgadas a lo largo del manto,

y cree que entiende por qué, aunque le molesta
que no me conmueve su necesidad de brillo.

Cree que me conoce, pero no puede conocerme.
No puede ver a través de mis ojos, y aunque realmente

deseo poder, no puedo escapar de mi cabeza y ponerme
cómodamente detrás de la cresta de su frente, ya sea tampoco.

Los mejores expertos en relaciones actuales insisten en que no debiéramos saber
todo acerca del otro. Dejar encendida la vela del misterio.

Aprender todo y arriesgar empaparse todos los fuegos de la pasión.
apoyarse demasiado cerca y correr el riesgo de ardiendo los fuegos.

Digo bien a todo esto. Demos mucho aire a nuestra vela.
Que arda caliente, ¿pero podemos cubrirla con una pantalla de lámpara?

— *Amy Baskin*
(traducción, T. Warburton y Bajo y rvb)

LJÓMA

'Uppskerutími' Edison LED ljósaperur sera augu mín og heila
að því marki þar sem ég þarf lyf til að virka og

sólgleraugu til að vafra mig um lifandi
heimurinn, stofan.

Félagi minn þekkir mig. Veit að ég mun taka mánuði
að ákveða málningarflögur og áklæðningarefni,

veit að ég vil frekar myrkrana með æðruleysi
árstíðabundin ljós strengd meðfram möttlinum með fáum lumenum,

og hann heldur að hann skilji af hverju, þó að það bitni á honum
að ég hreyðist ekki við þörf hans fyrir birtustig.

Hann heldur að hann þekki mig, en hann geti ekki þekkt mig.
Hann getur ekki séð í gegnum augu mín, og þó sannarlega

Ég vildi óska þess að ég gæti, get ekki sloppið við höfuðið og sest

þægilega á bak við hálsinn á enni sínu, heldur.

Núverandi sérfræðingar í efstu samböndum krefjast þess að við ættum
ekki að vita það
allt um hvert annað. Láttu leyndardómskertið loga.

Lærðu allt og hættu að svífa alla loga ástríðunnar.
Hallaðu of nærri og hættu að smeygja þeim loga.

Ég segi ágætlega við allt þetta. Við skulum gefa kertinu okkar nóg af lofti.
Má brenna það heitt, en - getum við hyljað það með lampaskermum?

— *Amy Baskin*
(Þýtt úr Ensku, Michael Lohr)

Astralna ločitev

Andrej Blatnik

Parček ob bazenu, utrujen od dolgočasnega dneva, si navdušeno izmenjuje obljube iz horoskopa. Kaj vse lepega jima napoveduje! Dolga ljubezen, veliko denarja, pridni otroci. To so res dobre počitnice, si mislita, dobro sva izbrala, kako naj bo drugače, dobra človeka sva, svet je pravičen.

A glej težavo, ki se jima bliža, nebo je ponagajalo ali pa je kaj pogoljufal astrolog, zmašil skupaj astralno napoved po prekrokani noči, ne da bi se ozrl v zvezde, kajti nikjer ne piše prava, nesrečna usoda: da bo čez nekaj minut enemu izmed vrtnarjev, ki bodo z električnimi škarjami obrezovali grmičevje ob bazenu, nesrečno spodrsnilo in se bo s škarjami vred znašel v vodi. Kjer se onadva ravno razigrano škropita in razmišljata, kako bi dala ime otroku, ki sta ga morda zaplodila včeraj.

Elektrika in voda, to se ne more končati dobro. Kričanje, sirene reševalcev, a ni kaj pomagati. Sledijo veliki naslovi v časopisih, ugibanje o malomarnosti zaradi slabega ravnanja, spraševanja, ali ne bi morale take škarje kdaj že končati na odpadu, odpovedi rezervacij, čez nekaj mesecev bodo morali hotel zapreti, ne bo pozabljeno, kot so upali lastniki.

Nihče ne bo vedel, da ni bil kriv astrolog, ki je napoved pripravil skrbno kot vselej, da je šlo v nebesih nekaj narobe, nekaj drugače od pričakovanj. Nobenih otrok ne bo in nobenega bogastva. Nebesa so včasih tako neurejena. *Q*

Astralna rastava

Andrej Blatnik
(Prijevod, Jagna Pogačnik)

Par kraj bazena, umoran od dosadnog dana, oduševljeno razmjenjuje obećanja iz horoskopa. Što im sve lijepog prognozira? Duga ljubav, puno novaca, dobra djeca. Ovo je doista dobar odmor, misle si, dobro smo izabrali, kako bi i bilo drukčije, dobri smo ljudi, svijet je pravedan.

No, eto problema koji im se približava, nebo je zadirkivalo ili je astrolog nešto prevario, skrpao astralnu prognozu nakon prolumpane noći, ne osvrčući se na zvijezde, jer nigdje ne piše prava, nesretna sudbina: da će se za nekoliko minuta jedan od vrtlara, koji će električnim škarama obrezivati grmlje kraj bazena, nesretno poskliznuti i skupa sa škarama naći u vodi. Gdje se ono dvoje upravo razigrano brćka i razmišlja kako će nazvati dijete koje su možda jučer začeli.

Struja i voda, to ne može završiti dobro. Vikanje, sirena hitne, ali nema pomoći. Slijede veliki naslovi u novinama, nagađanje o nemaru zbog lošeg upravljanja, pitanja ne bi li takve škare već jednom trebale završiti na otpadu, otkazivanja rezervacija, za nekoliko će mjeseci morati zatvoriti hotel, neće se zaboraviti kako su se to vlasnici nadali.

Nitko neće znati da nije bio kriv astrolog koji je prognozu pripremio brižno kao i uvijek, da je u nebesima nešto krenulo pogrešno, nešto drukčije od očekivanja. Neće biti nikakve djece i nikakvog bogatstva. Nebesa su ponekad tako nesređena. *Q*

Astralni razvod

Andrej Blatnik
(Prevod, Ivan Antić)

Simpatičan par kraj bazena, umoran od dosadnog dana, s oduševljenjem razmenjuje obećavajuće replike iz horoskopa. A šta im se sve tu lepo predviđa! Ljubav duga, para mnogo, deca dobra. Odličan je, bogami, ovaj naš godišnji, misle oni, dobro smo to izabrali, a kako bi drugačije bilo, dobri smo ljudi, a svet je pravedan.

Al' pazi sad kakva im se propast sprema, il' se nebo čika il' je astrolog, prevrtljivac, naškrabao astralnu prognozu nakon bančenja ne bacivši pogled na zvezde, kao, tobože, nigde se nije mogla pročitati prava, nesrećna sudbina: da će se za svega nekoliko minuta jedan od baštovana koji električnim makazama obrezuju grmlje kraj bazena, slučajno okliznuti i naći u vodi, s makazama. Baš tamo gde se njih dvoje razigrano škropuckaju i razmišljaju kako će dati ime detetu koje su, eto, možda baš juče začeli.

Struja i voda, to se ne može završiti srećno. Urlici, sirene ambulantskih kola, a pomoći nema. Uslediće krupni naslovi u novinama, nagađanje o nemarnosti usled lošeg rukovanja, pretresanje tema poput zar ne bi takve električne makaze morale već odavno biti na otpadu, zatim otkazivanje rezervacija, tako da se za nekoliko meseci morao zatvoriti hotel, nije sve to palo u zaborav, kako su se ponadali vlasnici.

I niko neće znati da astraolog, koji je horoskop napisao brižljivo kao i uvek, nije kriv, da je nešto krenulo naopako na samom nebu, nešto drukčije od očekivanog. Neće tu biti nikakve dece i neće tu biti nikakvog bogatstva. Nebo je ponekad, jašta, prilično loše uređeno. *Q*

Astral Separation

Andrej Blatnik
(Translation, Tamara M. Soban)

Tired out by the tediousness of the day, the couple by the pool eagerly read to each other what their horoscopes promise. What wonderful things are forecast! Long-lasting love, loads of money, good kids. This is one good vacation, they think, we've chosen well, but that's to be expected, we're good people, the world is just.

But lo and behold, trouble is looming; the heavens must have played a dirty trick, or else the astrologer has cheated, slapping together an astral prediction after a night on the booze without consulting the stars, because their real, adverse fate isn't written anywhere: A few minutes from now, one of the gardeners pruning a bush by the pool with an electric trimmer will slip so unfortunately he'll end up in the water, trimmer and all. In the water where right now they're playfully splashing each other and thinking about what to name the baby they may have conceived yesterday.

Electricity and water, that can't end well. Screams, ambulance sirens, but nothing to be done. Then come the banner headlines, speculations about negligence and malpractice, wonderings as to whether such trimmers shouldn't have been disused long ago, cancellations of reservations, and in a few months' time the hotel will have to close, the whole thing won't blow over as the owners will hope.

No one will ever know that it wasn't the astrologer's fault, that he had drawn up his prognoses as painstakingly as always, that something had gone wrong in the heavens, had gone against expectations. There will be no children and no prosperity. The heavens are sometimes so messy. *Q*

Астрална разделба

АНДРЕЈ БЛАТНИК

(Перевод, Лидија ДИмковска)

Една двојка крај базенот, изморени од здодевниот ден, одушевено си разменуваат ветувања од хороскопот. Колку само убави нешта им претскажуваат! Долга љубов, многу пари, добри деца. Ова е навистина добар одмор, си велат, добро избравме. Па како инаку, добри луѓе сме, светот е правичен.

Ама види ја ти несреќата што им се приближува, или небото се пошегувало со нив или ги измамил астрологот, набавтал некаква астрална прогноза по непроспиена ноќ, без да погледне во ѕвездите, зашто никаде не пишува вистинска, несреќна судбина: дека за некоја минута еден од градинарите кои со електрични ножици ги поткаструваат грмушките крај базенот, несреќно ќе се лизне и со ножиците ќе се бапне во водата. Таму каде што тие токму тогаш разиграно се прскаат и размислуваат какво име ќе му дадат на детето што можеби го зачнале вчера.

Струја и вода, тоа не може добро да заврши. Викотници, сирени на брзата помош, но им нема спас. Следуваат крупни наслови во весниците, нагаѓања за немарноста поради лошо постапување, прашања од типот зар не би требало таквите ножици веќе еднаш да завршат на отпад, откажување на резервациите, хотелот ќе треба да се затвори на неколку месеци, настанот нема да биде заборавен како што се надеваа сопствениците.

Никој нема да знае дека не бил виновен астрологот кој прогнозата ја подготвил грижливо како и секогаш, туку дека во небесата нешто наопаку излегло, нешто поинаку од очекувањата. Никакви деца нема да има и никакво богатство. Небесата понекогаш се толку несредени. *Q*

Separación astral

Andrej Blatnik

(Traducción, Marjeta Drobnič)

La parejita junto a la piscina, cansada del día aburrido, comparte con entusiasmo las promesas del horóscopo. ¡Les anuncia tantas cosas maravillosas! Un amor largo, mucho dinero, hijos obedientes. Estas son vacaciones más completas, piensan, hemos elegido bien, no podría ser de otra forma, somos buenas personas, el mundo es justo.

Pero mira la desgracia que se les acerca, el cielo se habría puesto travieso o el astrólogo habría hecho una trampa, una chapuza de la predicción astral después de una noche de juerga, sin haber consultado las estrellas, pues en ninguna parte pone nada que coincida con su mala suerte: dentro de unos minutos, uno de los jardineros que recortarán los arbustos al borde la piscina con las tijeras eléctricas resbalará infelizmente y caerá al agua junto con sus tijeras. Allí, donde, justo en este momento, ellos dos se salpican juguetones, pensando qué nombre ponerle al niño que quizás engendrasen ayer.

La electricidad y el agua, eso no puede terminar bien. Gritos, sirenas de ambulancias, pero no hay remedio. Lo que sigue son los grandes titulares en los periódicos, las conjeturas sobre la negligencia en la organización de trabajo, las preguntas si tales tijeras no deberían haber terminado ya antes en un vertedero, las anulaciones de las reservas, dentro de unos meses tendrán que cerrar el hotel, eso no se olvidará, como habrán esperado los dueños.

Nadie sabrá que el astrólogo, quien elaboró con meticulosidad su pronóstico, como lo hacía siempre, no tenía la culpa, que algo había fallado en el cielo, que había surgido algo contrario a las previsiones. No habrá niños ni riquezas. Los cielos son, a veces, tan desordenados. *Q*

Najbolj vznemirljivo

Andrej Blatnik

Ko jo terapevt vpraša, kaj jo je v življenju najbolj vznemirilo, dolgo molči. Nato reče, da se je njen mož nekoč peljal za parom na malem motorčku, rečejo jim vespe, se ji zdi. Bilo je soparno dolgo poletje in par se je očitno vračal s plaže. Izpod čelad jima je polzel pot, mož ji je pravil, da je vozil čisto blizu in videl te drobne potočke, kako so tekli po koži. Ženska, ki je sedela zadaj, je imela na sedež položeno pisano brisačo, bila sta v kopalkah, kopalke so bile majcene, tanke, ji je rekel mož, skoraj kot zobne nitke.

In potem se je tej ženski zgornji del kopalk odpel in z eno roko je lovila pobegla trakca, z drugo pa se je vendarle morala, da ne bi padla, držati svojega moškega, ki ni vedel, kaj se dogaja. Lovila je trakca in tenka črta na hrbtu ji je poplesavala sem ter tja, ni bilo veliko sončenja zgoraj brez to poletje, je sklepal njen mož, ko je pripovedoval o tej vožnji, in velikokrat je pripovedoval, v družbi ali samo njej, morda tudi samemu sebi, kadar ga dolgo ni bilo iz kopalnice, kdo bi vedel. Ampak potem sta nekam zavila, je rekel, in ni mogel povedati, ali je kopalke obdržala ali pa jih je odnesel veter. Moral bi voziti za njima, je včasih dodal, le v mislih, a ona je slišala.

In ta vožnja, o kateri je govoril njen mož, in ta pogled na hrbet te ženske, ki ji je zgornji del kopalk uhajal, to je bilo tisto najbolj vznemirljivo. O tem je velikokrat sanjala.

Tudi danes bo, nazadnje še reče, čisto tiho. Terapevt razumevajoče pokima. *Q*

Most Exciting

Andrej Blatnik

(Translation, Tamara M. Soban)

When her therapist asks what was the thing that excited her most in life, she's silent a long time. Then she says there was this time her husband was driving behind a couple on one of those little motorbikes, what they call a scooter, she thinks. It was a long, sweltering summer and the couple was obviously coming back from the beach. Sweat trickled down from under their helmets, her husband said he was driving real close behind and could see the tiny rivulets slithering down the skin. Riding pillion, the woman had a bright beach towel on the seat, they were both in bathing suits, the leather of the seats must burn if it's fake, and her bikini was teeny-weeny, skimpy, her husband said, hardly more than dental floss.

And then this woman's bikini top came undone and she tried to catch the fugitive strings with one hand while holding on to her man with the other; he had no idea what was going on. She tried to catch the flimsy strings, and the thin tan line on her back wiggled around, she couldn't have sunbathed topless much that summer, reasoned her husband when he talked about that ride, and he talked about it a lot, in company or just to her, perhaps also to himself when he took a long time coming out of the bathroom, who could say. But then they turned off the road, he said, and he couldn't say if she kept her bikini top or if it was blown off by the wind. I should've kept following them, he sometimes added, only in his mind, but she could hear him anyway.

That car ride her husband talked about, the view of that woman's back with the elusive bikini top—that was the most exciting thing ever. She's dreamed about it often. She'll also dream about it tonight, she says at last, very softly. Her therapist nods understandingly. *Q*

Највознемирувачкото

АНДРЕЈ БЛАТНИК

(Перевод, Лидийа ДИмковска)

Кога терапевтот ја прашува што ја вознемирило најмногу во животот, таа долго молчи. Потоа вели дека еднаш нејзиниот маж се возел зад една двојка на моторче, на веспа, така ѝ се чини. Било запурно, долго лето и двојката очигледно се враќала од плажа. Од под кацигите им течела пот, така маж ѝ ѝ кажувал, возел сосема блиску па ги видел тие ситни поточиња што им течеле по кожата. Жената седната назад имала ставено шарена крпа врз седиштето, биле во костими за капење, а нејзиниот бил малечок, тенок, ѝ рекол маж ѝ, речиси како конец за заби.

И потоа на жената ѝ се откопчал горниот дел и таа со едната рака почнала да ја бара побегнатата врвка, а со другата морала, за да не падне, да се држи за мажот кој не знаел што се случува. Ја пофаќала врвката додека тенката линија врз грбот ѝ играла овде-онде, а тоа лето немало многу сончање без горен дел, заклучил нејзиниот маж, кој многупати раскажувал за тоа возење, во друштво или само нејзе, можеби и самиот себеси кога долго го немало да излезе од бањата, којзнае. Ама потоа свртиле некаде, рекол, и не може да каже дали го задржала горниот дел од костимот за капење или ѝ го однел ветрот. Требаше да возам по нив, понекогаш ќе додал, само во мислите, но таа му ги имала слушнато.

И тоа возење за кое зборувал нејзиниот маж, и тој поглед врз плеќите на жената на која ѝ бегал горниот дел, тоа било највознемирувачкото. За тоа многупати и сонувала. И денес ќе сонува, најпосле вели, сосема тивко. Терапевтот кимнува со разбирање. *Q*

Najuznemirljivije

Andrej Blatnik

(Prijevod, Jagna Pogačnik)

Kad je terapeut pita što ju je u životu najviše uznemirilo, dugo šuti. Potom kaže da se njezin muž jednom vozio za parom na malom motociklu, zovu ih vespe čini joj se. Bilo je sparno dugačko ljeto i par se očito vraćao s plaže. Ispod kaciga curio im je znoj, muž joj je rekao da je vozio posve blizu i vidio te sitne potočiće kako su tekli po koži. Žena koja je sjedila iza, na sjedalu je imala šareni ručnik, bili su u kupaćima, kupaći su bili maleni, tanki, rekao joj je muž, skoro kao zubni konac.

I onda se toj ženi odvezao gornji dio kupaćeg i jednom je rukom hvatala odbjeglu trakicu, a drugom se ipak morala, da ne padne, držati svog muškarca koji nije znao što se događa. Lovila je trakicu i tanka crta na leđima plesala je amo i tamo, nije bilo puno sunčanja 'gore bez' toga ljeta, zaključio je njezin muž dok je pričao o toj vožnji, a često je pričao, u društvu ili samo njoj, možda i samome sebi kad ga nije bilo dugo iz kupaonice, tko bi znao. Ali onda su nekamo skrenuli, rekao je, i nije mogao reći je li zadržala kupaći ili ga je odnio vjetar. Trebao je voziti za njima, ponekad bi dodao samo u mislima, ali ona je čula.

I ta vožnja, o kojoj je govorio njezin muž, i taj pogled na leđa te žene kojoj je bježao gornji dio kupaćeg, to je bilo ono najuznemirljivije. O tome je često sanjala. I danas će, kaže na kraju, osve tiho. Terapeut kimne s razumijevanjem. *Q*

Najuznemirljivije

Andrej Blatnik
(Prevod, Ivan Antić)

Kada ju je terapeut upitao šta je to što je najviše uzbudilo u životu, ona je najpre dugo ćutala. A onda reče da je jednom prilikom njen muž bio u autu iza para na malom motoru, zovu se vespe, čini joj se. Beše dugo sparno leto i par se, po svemu sudeći, vraćao s plaže. Kapljice znoja curele su im pod kacigama, rekao joj je da je vozio tako blizu da je mogao videti malene potočiće kako teku niz kožu. Žena, koja je bila pozadi, sedela je na šarenom peškiru prebačenom preko sedišta, i oboje su na sebi imali samo kupaće, a njen je kupaći bio malen i tanušan, rekao je njen muž, gotovo kao konac za zube.

I onda se taj njen gornji deo kupaćeg odvezao i ona je jednom rukom pokušavala da uhvati tračicu dok se drugom, svakako, kako ne bi pala, morala držati za muškarca koji nije ni slutio šta se iza događa. Ganjala je tračicu i tanka crta na leđima lepršala je tamo-amo; nije bilo previše sunčanja tog leta, zaključio je njen muž dok je pričao o toj vožnji, a mnogo puta je pričao, u društvu ili samo njoj, možda i samom sebi kad bi se zadržao duže u kupatilu, ko bi ga znao. Ali posle su negde skrenuli, rekao je, tako da ne bi mogao da tvrdi da li je gornji deo ostao na njoj ili ga je odneo vetar. Trebalo je da krene za njima, dodao bi ponekad, ali samo u mislima, no ona bi to čula.

I ta vožnja o kojoj je govorio njen muž, i taj pogled na leđa žene kojoj gornji deo kupaćeg izmiče, to je bilo ono što ju je najviše uznemirilo. To je mnogo puta sanjala. I danas će biti, reče ona na kraju, sasvim tiho. Terapeut klimnu glavom, u znak razumevanja. *Q*

Lo más inquietante

Andrej Blatnik
(Traducción, Marjeta Drobnič)

Cuando el terapeuta le pregunta qué ha sido lo que más la ha inquietado en su vida, se queda callada durante mucho tiempo. Después dice que una vez su marido iba conduciendo detrás de una pareja en una moto pequeña, que, le parece, llamaban Vespa. Era un verano largo y bochornoso y, por lo visto, la pareja volvía de la playa. Por debajo de los cascos les rezumaba el sudor, su marido le contaba que les había seguido muy de cerca y había podido ver aquellos arroyitos diminutos chorreando por sus pieles. La mujer, que iba detrás, tenía una toalla de colores puesta a través del asiento, llevaban bañador y bikini, prendas minúsculas, delgadas, le decía su marido, casi como hilos dentales.

Y, después, a la mujer se le desabrochó la parte superior del bikini, y mientras con una mano trataba de atrapar las fugadas tiras, con la otra, sin más remedio, seguía agarrándose de su hombre para no caerse, sin que él se hubiera dado cuenta de lo que pasaba. Intentaba atrapar las tiras y una línea delgada en su espalda bailaba de un lado a otro, no se veía mucho bronceado *topless* aquel verano, razonaba su marido cuando contaba acerca de aquel trayecto, y lo contaba muchas veces, en compañía o sólo a ella, tal vez también a sí mismo cuando tardaba en salir del baño, quién podría saberlo. Pero después giraron, dijo, y no sabía decir si ella había conservado su bikini o si se lo había llevado el viento. Debería haberlos seguido, añadía a veces, sólo mentalmente, pero ella lo oía.

Y aquel trayecto del que contaba su marido, y aquella visión de la espalda de la mujer a la que se le iba la parte superior del bikini, aquella fue la cosa lo más inquietante. Ha soñado muchas veces con ella. Y soñará con esa esta noche, concluye al fin, en voz muy baja. El terapeuta asiente comprensivamente. *Q*

Blade Runner 2049, de Denis Villeneuve: Cuatro preguntas y cuatro hipótesis para pensar *Blade Runner 2049*

Aarón Rodríguez

01: La primera pregunta: ¿Desde dónde se mira una imagen?

La imagen se mira siempre desde uno mismo y desde su tiempo. Quizá la única crítica posible sobre *Blade Runner 2049* —la única que pudiera correr más rápido que su propio recuerdo, que los visionados anteriores de la propia película de Scott— sería aquella imposible experiencia de un espectador virgen, un espectador al que se le permitiera quizá conocer los mitos y los dioses, pero no el texto inicial, ni ninguno de los interminables montajes del director que han ido surgiendo, año tras año, en la cartelera.

Četiri pitanja i četiri hipoteze za razmišljanje o filmu *Blade Runner 2049* Denisa Villeneuvea

Aarón Rodríguez
(Prijevod s engleskog, Ana Katana)

01: Prvo pitanje: Iz koje točke gledišta promatraš sliku?

Slika se uvijek gleda iz nečije perspektive, i nečijeg razdoblja. Možda je jedina moguća kritika na račun *Blade Runnera 2049* - jedina koja bi mogla nadvladati vaše sjećanje, ako izuzmemo prethodna gledanja Scottova izvornika – ono nemoguće iskustvo Djevičanskog gledatelja, onoga kojemu je možda dopušten uvid u mitove i bogove, ali ne u početni tekst, ili ijedan od Scottovih beskrajnih uradaka koji se godinu za godinom pojavljuju na velikim plakatima.

La primera hipótesis: Quizá, si escucháramos a este espectador virgen, quedaríamos defraudados.

Prva hipoteza: kad bismo poslušali djevičanskog gledatelja, možda bismo se razočarali.

Four Questions & Four Hypotheses for Pondering Denis Villeneuve's *Blade Runner 2049*

Aarón Rodríguez
(English tr. fr. the Spanish, rvb)

01: A first question: From what vantage point do you look at an image?

The image is always seen from someone's perspective, and from their time period. Perhaps the only possible criticism about *Blade Runner 2049*—the only one that could outrun your own memory, other than previous viewings of Scott's original film—would be the impossible experience of a *Virgin Spectator,* a spectator who might be allowed to learn of myths and gods, but not of the initial text, or of any of Scott's endless tinkered assemblages that emerged on billboards year after year.

Fjórir spurningar og fjórar tilgátur til að hugleiða Blade Runner 2049 is Denis Villeneuve

Aarón Rodríguez
(Þýtt úr Ensku, Michael Lohr)

01: Fyrsta spurning: Frá hvaða sjónarhóli lítur þú á mynd?

Myndin er alltaf litið á frá sjónarhóli einhvers og frá tímabils viðkomandi. Kannski er eina mögulega gagnrýniin um Blade Runner 2049, sú eina sem gæti runnið út eigin minni, annað en fyrri sýn á upprunalegu kvikmynd Scott, sem er ómöguleg reynsla af Virgin Áhorfandi, áhorfandi sem gæti fengið að læra af goðsögnum og guðir, en ekki af fyrstu textanum, eða einhverju af endalausum samningum Scott sem kom fram á auglýsingaskilti ár eftir ár.

A first hypothesis: Listening to this virgin spectator, we'd perhaps be disappointed.

Fyrsta tilgátu: Ef við hlustum á þennan meysku áhorfanda gætum við verið fyrir vonbrigðum.

02 La segunda pregunta: ¿Qué significa "pensar una imagen"?

Desde hace unos años, el profesor Josep María Català lleva explorando la posibilidad de "pensar a través de las imágenes", un paso previo ya esbozado por Deleuze que nos permitiría, por cierto, escapar de los tics de las comparaciones entre cine y lenguaje. Si tomamos la imagen en su pureza, quizá podemos rastrear una cierta idea, un cierto decir sobre el mundo que únicamente puede compensarse en términos de complejidad, de atmósfera, de indefinición. Las imágenes —Daney lo dejó escrito una y mil veces— son siempre plurisignificantes, y por lo tanto, responden de manera sensiblemente diferente a cada uno de los espectadores.

Blade Runner 2049, empecemos por aquí, me impresiona como ese ejercicio de "pensamiento en imágenes". Tomemos como ejemplo la escena en la que la inteligencia artificial y un cuerpo femenino deben fusionarse en una única entidad para poder hacer el amor. La potencia de esos dos rostros que no terminan de unirse, de esos gestos apasionados que no terminan de

02: Drugo pitanje: Što se misli pod "misli sliku"?

Nekoliko je godina profesor Josep María Català istraživao mogućnost "razmišljanja putem slika", koraka koji je ranije opisao Deleuze, a koji nam omogućava izbjegavanje filmskih i jezičnih tikova. Ako prihvatimo sliku u njezinoj čistoći, možda možemo ući u trag nekoj ideji, aksiomu o svijetu koji se može pojmiti isključivo u terminima kompleksnosti, atmosfere, *nedefiniranosti.* Te slike – kako je Dany tisuću puta napisao – uvijek su *plurisignifikantne,* te stoga svaki pojedini gledatelj bitno drugačije reagira na svaku pojedinu sliku.

Blade Runner 2049 dojmio me se kao vježba "misli u slikama". Na primjer, u sceni gdje se umjetna inteligencija i tijelo žene moraju stopiti u jedno kako bi vodili ljubav. Snaga tih dvaju lica koja se ne mogu posve ujediniti, pokreta punih strasti koji kao da se međusobno ne uklapaju, postaje izvanredno precizna formulacija nepojmljive, vječito da-

02: A second question: What's meant by *"think an image"*?

For a few years, Professor Josep María Català has explored the possibility of *"thinking through images"* (previously outlined by Deleuze) that allows us, incidentally, to escape the tics of film and language. If we take the image in its purity, we can trace a certain idea, a certain axiom about the world that can only be thought of in terms of complexity, of atmosphere, of *indefinition*. These images—Daney wrote a thousand times—are always *plurisignifications*, and therefore each spectator has significantly different responses to each image.

02: Önnur spurning: Hvað er átt við með "hugsa mynd"?

Fyrir nokkrum árum hefur prófessor Josep María Català kannað möguleika á að "hugsa í gegnum myndir", skref sem áður var lýst af Deleuze sem gerir okkur kleift að komast hjá tics kvikmynda og tungumáls. Ef við tökum myndina í hreinleika, gætum við kannski rakið ákveðna hugmynd, ákveðin axiom um heiminn sem aðeins er hægt að hugsa um hvað varðar margbreytileika, andrúmsloft, óákvörðun. Þessar myndir - Daney skrifaði þúsund sinnum - er alltaf plurisignifications, og því hefur áhorfandinn verulega mismunandi svör við hverri mynd.

Blade Runner 2049 strikes me as a *"thought in images"* exercise. For example, the scene where an artificial intelligence must merge with a woman's body into a single entity in order to make love. The power of those two faces not quite uniting, of those passionate gestures not quite fitting, becomes an extraordinarily precise formulation of the unfathomable, always distant, nature of desire.

Blade Runner 2049 slær mig sem "hugsun í myndum" æfingu. Til dæmis er vettvangurinn þar sem gervigreind og líkami konunnar verður sameinað í einum aðila til að öðlast ást. Krafturinn á þessum tveimur andlitum, sem ekki er alveg sameinað, af þeim ástríðufullum bendingum sem ekki passa alveg, verða óvenju nákvæmlega mótun ófriðanlegrar, fjarlægðar eðlis

encajar, es una formulación extraordinariamente precisa de la naturaleza ajena, inaprehensible, siempre distante, del deseo. Un segundo ejemplo: la manera en la que, durante el prólogo, se disponen los sonidos —el burbujeo de una cacerola, los pasos sobre la madera, cada uno de los golpes propinados— genera una sinfonía deliciosa, una cierta atmósfera propicia a la ensoñación que otorga un perfecto tono para el resto de la cinta. Un tercer ejemplo: la manera en la que la creadora de recuerdos construye, con cuidado y mimo, un cumpleaños nunca vivido en el que cada sombra, cada centelleo de la vela, cada distancia entre los cuerpos infantiles, parece superponer matices riquísimos, de extraordinaria complejidad. Son tres pensamientos, pero en *Blade Runner 2049* hay muchos, muchos más.

La segunda hipótesis: Una suma de pensamientos extraordinarios, si no están hilados con coherencia, no tienen por qué desembocar en un discurso emocionante. Lo mismo puede decirse de las imágenes.

03 La tercera pregunta: ¿Cómo escribe aquí Denis Villeneuve?

En ciertos foros, su cine ha sido desechado con un gesto de desdén al considerar, de un plumazo, que sus películas eran mercadotecnia barata y efectismo

leke prirode požude. Drugi primjer: orkestracija zvukova u prologu - lonac koji krčka na štednjaku, koraci na drvenim gredama, svaki zadani udarac u borbi do smrti – sve to stvara slasnu simfoniju, snenu atmosferu koja zadaje savršen ton za ostatak filma. Treći primjer: način na koji je tvorac usađenih sjećanja koreografirao izmišljenu rođendansku zabavu, pomno podražavajući svaku sjenu, svaki treptaj svijeće, svaku udaljenost između dječjih tijela, podvrgavajući ih tako bogatim nijansama izvanredne kompleksnosti. Ovo su tek tri slike/ misli, no u filmu *Blade Runner 2049* ima ih mnogo, mnogo više.

Druga hipoteza: zbroj neobičnih misli neće uvijek dovesti do zanimljivog razgovora, ako se njime koherentno ne upravlja. Isto vrijedi i za slike.

03: Treće pitanje: Kako Denis Villeneuve ovdje piše?

Na nekim je forumima njegovo stvaralaštvo prezreno, a njegovi uradci smatrani jeftinim marketingom i suvišnim senzacionalizmom čija je namjena dodvoravanje masama, koje će zauzvrat napustiti kino osjećaju-

A second example: the way in which, during the prologue, sounds are orchestrated—a casserole's bubbling on the stove, footsteps on wood, each blow inflicted during a fight to the death—generates a delectable symphony, an atmosphere conducive to dreaming that sets a perfect tone for the rest of the film. A third example: the way in which the creator of implanted memories choreographs an imagined birthday party, miming with care every shadow, every twinkle of the candle, every distance between children's bodies, superimposing rich nuances of extraordinary complexity. These are three images/ thoughts, but in *Blade Runner 2049* there are many more.

A second hypothesis: a sum of extraordinary thoughts, if not spun coherently, doesn't always lead to exciting discourse. The same can be said of images.

03: A third question: How is Denis Villeneuve's writing here?

In certain forums, his cinema's been cast aside with disdain, considering, at a stroke, that his films were no more than cheap marketing and gratuitous sensationalism to impress the movie-going masses who, actually, came out of the cineplex feeling they'd opted for the pleasures of high culture.

löngunarinnar. Annað dæmi: hvernig í hljóði eru hljómar hljómar í hljómsveitinni, kúla á kápunni, fótspor á tré, hvert blása sem valdið er í baráttunni til dauða, býr til ástúðlegan symphony, andrúmsloft sem stuðlar að því að dreyma sem setur fullkomin tón fyrir afganginn af myndinni. Þriðja dæmi: hvernig skapandi ígræddar minningar sitja í ímyndaða afmælisveislu, miming með varúð hverri skuggi, hvert augnablik af kerti, hverri fjarlægð milli líkama barnsins og leggur mikla blæbrigði af ótrúlegum flækjum. Þetta eru þrjár myndir / hugsanir, en í Blade Runner 2049 eru fleiri, margt fleira.

Önnur tilgáta: Sumar óvenjulegar hugsanir, ef þau eru ekki spunnin samhliða, leiða ekki alltaf til spennandi umræðu. Sama má segja um myndir.

03: Þriðja spurning: Hvernig skrifar Denis Villeneuve hér?

Á ákveðnum vettvangi hefur kvikmyndahús hans verið kastað til hliðsjónar með því að hafa í huga að kvikmyndir hans voru ódýr markaðssetning og óréttmæt stórkostlegur til að vekja hrifningu á fjöldanum sem þvert á móti kom út úr leikhúsinu sem

gratuito para epatar a las grandes masas que, a la contra, salían de su cine con una cierta sensación de haber optado a los placeres de la alta cultura. Más allá del clasismo implícito en esta afirmación, lo cierto es que Villeneuve (o su escritura) encarna un cierto gesto contemporáneo del cine que puede superponerse, con matices y muchas diferencias, a los textos que filman en paralelo Nolan, Aronofsky, Fincher y algún otro. Lo que molesta no es el gesto —el gesto hay que pensarlo, y para ello hay que analizar con calma las películas— sino la fascinación de las masas.

El problema de *Blade Runner 2049* es que las masas ya venían fascinadas de casa, pero con un cuchillo bien afilado escondido tras la espalda. De ahí que las imágenes respondan a esa fascinación y, muchas veces, intenten sobrepasarla. El *tour de force* resulta insostenible por una razón muy sencilla: Los más de 150 minutos que dura la película. Cuando llegamos a la conclusión, en la que se pretende una depuración, una variación (no demasiado elaborada) sobre el final anterior de Scott (el agua, las lágrimas en la lluvia, por la nieve), estamos exhaustos de iluminaciones barrocas y composiciones extraordinarias. El gesto final, que podría conmover por su aparente sencillez, queda opacado por el propio peso con el que están compuestos todos los planos anteriores de la película.

ći se kulturno uzdignutima. Pored klasizma koji se dade naslutiti u ovoj izjavi, nalazi se i istina da Villeneuve (ili njegovo pisanje) utjelovljuje jednu vrstu suvremene kinematografske geste koja se može nametnuti, naravno uz nijanse i mnoge razlike, uz bok Nolanu, Aronofskom, Fincheru i drugima. Gesta nam nije trn u oku – o gesti se razmišlja, i stoga filmove analiziramo mirno – nama smeta masovna fascinacija. Problem *Blade Runnera 2049* je taj da mase dolaze u kino već fascinirane, s isukanim bodežima. Budući da slike odgovaraju toj fascinaciji, i mnogo puta je čak pokušavaju nadvladati, taj *tour de force* postaje neizdrživ iz jednog jednostavnog razloga: više od 150 minuta trajanja filma. Kad napokon dosegnemo zaključak i točku razjašnjenja (koja nije komplicirana), inačicu Scottova kraja (voda, suze na kiši, snijeg), barokni akcenti i izvanredne kompozicije već su nas iscrpili. Konačna gesta koja bi mogla biti nadasve dirljiva u svojoj jednostavnosti, zatomljena je velikom težinom svih ostalih razina filma.

Beyond the classism implicit in this statement, the truth is that Villeneuve (or his script) embodies a certain contemporary gesture of cinema that superimposes, with nuances and many differences, scenes that parallel Nolan, Aronofsky, Fincher and others. What bothers us isn't the gesture—the gesture has to be thought about, and for this we should analyze the films calmly—it's the masses' fascination.

The problem with *Blade Runner 2049* is that the masses came, and they saw, knives out. Hence the images respond to this fascination and, many times, try to overcome it. The *tour de force* becomes untenable for a very simple reason: the film's 150 plus minutes' length. When we reach the conclusion, where it aims at a clarification, a variation (not too elaborate) of the previous Scott ending (the water, tears in the rain, in the snow), the baroque highlights and the extraordinary compositions exhaust us. The final gesture, which could be moving in its apparent simplicity, is overshadowed by the very weight of all the previous planes of the film.

þeir höfðu valið fyrir ánægju af mikilli menningu. Beyond classism óneitanlega í þessari yfirlýsingu, sannleikurinn er sú að Villeneuve (eða handritið hans) felur í sér ákveðna nútíma hreyfingu kvikmyndagerðar sem hægt er að yfirbuga, með blæbrigði og margbreytileika, tjöldin sem samsíða Nolan, Aronofsky, Fincher og aðrir. Það sem kemur í veg fyrir okkur er ekki bendingin - það þarf að hugsa um bendinguna, og við ættum að greina kvikmyndirnar rólega - það er heillandi fjöldinn.

Vandamálið með *Blade Runner 2049* er að massarnir komu þegar heillaðir, hnífar tilbúnir. Þess vegna bregðast myndin við þessa heillun og reynir oft að sigrast á henni. Ferðin de þróttur verður óviðunandi af mjög einföldum ástæðu: 150 plús lengd myndarinnar. Þegar við komumst að þeirri niðurstöðu, þar sem það miðar að skýringu, breyting (ekki of vandaður) af fyrri Scott endingu (vatnið, tárin í rigningunni, í snjónum), barokk hápunktur og ótrúlega samsetningar útblástur okkur. Endanleg bending, sem gæti verið að flytja í augljósri einfaldleika, er skyggður af miklum þyngd allra fyrri flugvéla kvikmyndarinnar.

Si sobreponemos —quizá no sea muy descabellado— el final de *Blade Runner 2049* contra el chispazo abrasivo que cerraba *Enemy* (2013) o contra ese aullido brutal que nos arrasaba en *Incendies* (2010), quizá estamos algo más cerca de ver lo que Villeneuve ha perdido en su escritura. Aquí el peso de la dirección de arte es opresiva, moviéndose en una línea tan deslumbrantemente bella que termina por cegar. Tomemos los interiores en esa especie de pirámide de oro y agua (casi) bendita en la que habita Wallace. O los exteriores monstruosos de Las Vegas, con esas terribles mujeres gigantescas congeladas en un gesto de placer desmesurado. Villeneuve sabe cómo encuadrar, sabe cómo componer y cómo mover la cámara para que el espacio nos deslumbre y nos aplaste contra la butaca. La experiencia cinematográfica se impone por la vía de lo sublime. Pero el momento irrepetible del descubrimiento —eso que ocurría con la araña de *Enemy*, por así decirlo—, aquí parece haberse perdido.

La tercera hipótesis: Lo sublime puede imponerse, y en las manos correctas, puede deslumbrar e incluso resultar inolvidable. La belleza no puede imponerse.

Ako usporedimo kraj *Blade Runnera 2049* sa uništavajućom iskrom *Neprijatelja* (2013) ili sa brutalnim, razarajućim vriskom u *Našoj majci* (2010), možda ćemo se ponešto približiti onome što je Villeneuve izgubio tijekom pisanja. Ovdje je težina umjetničkog redateljstva tako napadna, a ujedno i toliko zasljepljujuće prekrasna, da nam na kraju ostane samo sljepilo. Uzmimo Wallaceovo piramidalno obitavalište, puno zlata i zamalo svete vode. Ili monstrouzne lasvegaške eksterijere, s onim zastrašujućim gigantskim ženama ukočenim u pokretima neizrecivih užitaka. Villeneuve zna kadrirati i kretati se kamerom tako da nas prostor zapanji i prilijepi za naslonjače. Filmsko iskustvo protkano je uzvišenošću. Ali neponovljivi trenutak otkrivenja –onaj sa paukom u *Neprijatelju*, na primjer – kao da nam je promaknuo.

Treća hipoteza: uzvišenost može prevagnuti, i čak biti blještava i nezaboravna u pravim rukama. Ljepota ne može prevagnuti.

If we overlay *Blade Runner 2049's* ending on the abrasive spark that closes *Enemy* (2013) or on that brutal razing howl in *Incendies* (2010), we might be a little closer to seeing what Villeneuve's lost in his script. Here the art direction's weight is oppressive, moving in a line so blindly beautiful that it ends up only being blinding. Let's take Wallace's pyramid dwelling with its interiors of gold and beatific water. Or the monstrous Las Vegas exteriors, with terrible gigantic women frozen in gestures of untold pleasure. Villeneuve knows how to frame, how to compose and how to move the camera so that space dazzles and crushes us against our armchairs. The film experience is imposed by the sublime. But the unrepeatable moment of discovery—such as the one with the Enemy Spider, let's say—seems to have been lost.

A third hypothesis: the sublime can prevail, and in the right hands, can dazzle and even be unforgettable. Beauty cannot prevail.

Ef við leggjum yfir lok *Blade Runner 2049* á slípiefni sem lokar *Óvinur* (2013) eða á því grimmdri razing í *Incendies* (2010), gætum við verið nálægt því að sjá hvað Villeneuve hefur misst í handritinu. Hér er þyngd listalífsins kúgandi og hreyfist í línu sem er svo blindu falleg að það endar aðeins að vera blindandi. Við skulum taka pýramída Wallace með innréttingum sínum af gulli og næstum blessuðu vatni. Eða hinn mikli Las Vegas utanríkisráðherra, með þeim hræðilegu risastórum konum sem frosnir eru í athafnir af óeðlilegum ánægju. Villeneuve veit hvernig á að ramma, hvernig á að búa saman og hvernig á að færa myndavélina þannig að plássið muni glæða og mylja okkur gegn hægindastólunum okkar. Kvikmyndaleynslan er lögð af háleitri. En aldrei endurtaka augnablik uppgötvuneins og sá með Óvinurinn Kónguló, segjum, virðist hafa misst.

Þriðja tilgáta: háleitið getur sigrað og í rétta hendur getur blönduð og jafnvel verið ógleymanleg. Fegurð getur ekki sigrað.

04 La cuarta pregunta: ¿Es una buena película?

Es la pregunta más compleja, y por otro lado, la que quizá todo lector espera que una crítica responda. Sin embargo, sería más inteligente señalar que es una película compleja en el mejor sentido de la palabra. Lo es porque está compuesta de decenas de capas significantes —el perro que nunca sabremos si es o no real, la falsa resurrección de Rachel— que se despliegan de manera ordenada en un ejercicio de *zapping*. Lo es también porque sus imágenes están minuciosamente construidas, fabricadas con la sólida, narcisista y apabullante voluntad de permanecer en nuestra memoria a toda costa —habrá quien considere esto un rasgo negativo, pero yo no lo haré—. Es una película compleja porque ofrece muchos pensamientos envueltos en muchas imágenes.

Su problema es, precisamente, que la hilazón no forma trama, es decir, que si nos alejamos del punto de vista microanalítico e intentamos contemplar el fresco, el tapiz total de lo que se piensa en *Blade Runner 2049* veremos que no podemos llegar muy lejos. La película original de Scott era una lección tozuda de filosofía que se dirigía en una única dirección a esbozar dos o tres preguntas a medio camino entre Descartes y una naciente Filosofía de la Mente. Su potencia residía en la manera en la que generaba un arquitrabe conceptual —especial-

04: Četvrto pitanje: je li ovo dobar film?

To je najkompleksnije, najsloženije pitanje, a s druge strane, svaki čitatelj očekuje upravo odgovor na njega. No najpametnije bi bilo ukazati na činjenicu kako je ovo kompleksan film u najboljem smislu te riječi. Složen je od niza značajnih slojeva – pas koji jeste, ili možda nije stvaran, Rachelino lažno uskrsnuće – koji se uredno postavljaju u hitru vježbu. Slike su pomno i minuciozno izrađene, sa čvrstom, narcističkom, nametljivom namjerom da ostanu upamćene po svaku cijenu. Neki bi to možda smatrali negativnim, ali ne ja. To je kompleksan film jer nudi mnoštvo misli omotano mnoštvom slika.

Villeneuveov problem je upravo to; tkanje misli nije razvijanje radnje. Ako se odmaknemo od mikroanalitičkog gledišta i pokušamo razmotriti cijelu tapiseriju misli u *Blade Runneru 2049,* otkrivamo da nećemo daleko stići. Scottov izvornik bio je tvrdokorna lekcija iz filozofije temeljena na nekoliko pitanja na pola puta između Descartesa i nove škole mišljenja. Njegova moć ležala je u načinu stvaranja konceptualnog arhitrava - pogotovo u posljednjem, proslavljenom

04: A fourth question: is it a *good* film?

It's the most complex, even complicated question, and one that, on the other hand, readers expect criticism to answer. It might be wiser to point out that it's a complex film in the best sense of the word. This is because it's composed of dozens of significant layers—the dog that may or may not be real, Rachel's fake resurrection—that unfold in an orderly fashion into a kind of zapping exercise. And because its images are painstakingly built, manufactured with a solidity, a narcissistic and overwhelming will to remain in our memory at all costs. Some consider this a negative trait, but I don't. It's a complex film because it offers many thoughts wrapped in many images.

Villeneuve's problem is precisely that the weave isn't a plot; that is, if we move away from the microanalytic point of view and try to contemplate the total tapestry of thought in *Blade Runner 2049* we find we can't go far. Scott's original film was a stubborn lesson in philosophy that was directed at a few questions poised halfway between Descartes and a nascent philosophy of mind. Its potency lay in the way it generated a conceptual architrave—especially in its last and celebrated sequence—be-

04: Fjórða smellu í andlitið: er það góð kvikmynd?

Það er flóknasta, jafnvel flókin spurningin og sú sem hins vegar flestir lesendur búast við gagnrýni til að svara. Það væri hins vegar vitur að benda á að það sé flókið kvikmynd í besta skilningi orðsins. Það er vegna þess að það samanstendur af heilmikið af verulegum lögum, hundurinn sem mega eða mega ekki vera raunverulegur, falsa upprisu Rachel, sem þróast á réttan hátt í nokkurs konar zapping æfingu. Það er líka vegna þess að myndirnar hennar eru vandlega byggð, framleidd með traustum, narcissistic og yfirgnæfandi vilja til að vera í minni okkar að öllum kostnaði. Sumir kunna að líta á þetta sem neikvæð einkenni, en ég geri það ekki. Það er flókið kvikmynd vegna þess að það býður upp á margar hugsanir umbúðir í mörgum myndum.

Vandamál Villeneuve er einmitt að vefnaðurinn er ekki samsæri; Það er ef við förum í burtu frá örfræðilegu sjónarhóli og reynum að hugleiða heildarhugsunina í Blade Runner 2049 við sjáum að við getum ekki farið langt. Upprunalega kvikmyndin í Scott var þrjóskur lexía í heimspeki sem var beint til nokkurra spurninga sem höfðu komið fyrir hálfa leið milli Descartes og hugsunarhugmyndarinnar. Virkni þess lá í því hvernig hún myndaði hugmyndafræðilega architrave-sérstaklega í síðasta og

mente en su última y célebre secuencia— entre mito, ciencia y teoría del conocimiento. Era una película controlada en sus conceptos.

Su secuela quiere pensar por encima de la filosofía, acudiendo directamente a la fuerza del plano visual, pero se queda en el truco de magia hipnotista. Al final, el relato no deja de ser una cuestión identitaria con tintes familiares más bien intrascendente. La hipotética revolución ocurre fuera de plano. Volviendo a Deleuze —ahora con Guattari—, no es sino una película sobre lo de siempre: "el sucio secretito de familia".

Repitamos, pues, la cuarta pregunta: ¿Es una buena película?

Frente a la crítica mayoritaria que está celebrando una suerte de epifanía poco menos que teológica al hilo de sus imágenes, me permitirán que yo adopte una postura mucho más humilde y les pida, por el contrario, paciencia y tiempo para juzgar bien lo que en la película se piensa y cómo se piensa. Necesitamos distancia, necesitamos imponer una cierta disciplina crítica sobre ella, necesitamos volver a verla cuando esté ya pasada de moda y nadie se sienta éticamente obligado a dar su opinión.

Ahí va la cuarta hipótesis: puede entonces que nuestro propio juicio decepcione a la película, pero sea, entonces, un juicio justo. *Q*

kadru – između mita, znanosti i teorije znanja. Taj je film vješto upravljao svojim konceptima.

Villeneuveov nastavak želi nadići filozofiju i krenuti ravno na vizualni plan, no zapeo je negdje u zupčanicima hipnotizerske čarolije. Na kraju, sve se svede na priču o pitanju identiteta sa poprilično nedosljednim blaćenjem vlastite obitelji. Hipotetička revolucija ostaje van scene. Vraćamo se Deleuzeu – sada i Guattariju – dobili smo samo uobičajen filmić o „prljavoj obiteljskoj tajni".

Dakle, ponavljam četvrto pitanje, je li ovo dobar film?

Suočen s većinom kritika koje slave taj niz slika kao neku vrstu navještenja koja graniči s teologijom, ja ću zauzeti mnogo skromniji položaj i zatražiti još vremena i strpljenja kako bih pravedno procijenio o čemu je ovaj film, i kako obrađuje svoju temu. Treba nam odmak, trebamo primijeniti određenu kritičku disciplinu, trebamo ga ponovno pogledati kad se slegne prašina i kad se nitko neće osjećati moralno obveznim iznijeti svoje mišljenje.

Evo četvrte hipoteze: možda će naša vlastita prosudba film proglasiti razočaravajućim, i možda je ta prosudba sasvim dovoljna. *Q*

tween myth, science and theory of knowledge. It was a film in control of its concepts.

Villeneuve's sequel wants to operate beyond philosophy, going directly to the power of the visual plane, but it's trapped in the gimmick of a hypnotist's magic. In the end, the story remains an identity issue with some rather inconsequential family shading. The hypothetical revolution occurs off-stage. Returning to Deleuze—now with Guattari—it's nothing but a movie about the usual: *"dirty little family secret."*

Let's repeat the fourth question: is it a good film?

Faced with the majority criticism that celebrates a sort of epiphany not much short of theological in its thread of images, let me adopt a much more humble position and ask, on the contrary, for the patience and the time to properly judge what the film is dealing with, and how it deals with it. We need distance, and to impose a certain critical discipline, and to see it again when the dust settles and no one feels an ethical obligation to give an opinion.

Here's the fourth hypothesis: if our own judgment may then find the film disappointing, that judgement may be fair enough. *Q*

haldinri röð milli mýtu, vísinda og kenningar um þekkingu. Það var kvikmynd sem stjórnaði hugmyndum sínum.

Framhald Villeneuve vill starfa út fyrir heimspeki, fara beint í kraft sjónrænu planarinnar, en það er föst í gimmick galdrahyggjunnar. Í lokin er sagan ennþá einkenni vandamál með nokkuð frekar ósvikin fjölskylduskygging. Hugsanlega byltingin er utan stigs. Aftur á Deleuze-nú með Guattari-það er ekkert annað en kvikmynd um venjulega: "óhreint lítið fjölskyldu leyndarmál."

Svo við skulum endurtaka fjórða spurninguna: er það góð kvikmynd? Frammi fyrir meiriháttar gagnrýni sem fagnar einni tegund af epiphany sem er ekki mjög stutt af guðfræðilegri í þræði myndanna, leyfðu mér að samþykkja miklu auðmjúkari stöðu og spyrðu þvert á móti um þolinmæði og tíma til að dæma réttilega hvað kvikmyndin er að takast á við með, og hvernig það fjallar um það. Við þurfum fjarlægð, við þurfum að setja ákveðna gagnrýni, við þurfum að sjá það aftur þegar rykið setur og enginn telur siðferðilega skyldu að gefa álit.

Hér er fjórða tilgátan: eigin dómur okkar getur þá fundið myndina vonbrigðum og þessi dómur getur verið sanngjörn. *Q*

Air

~Inhale~

There's a small frame from the time the air leaves the lungs. Reaching deep into each alveoli bed. Pulling up each element in the pockets. Coursing through our blood cells to oxygenate us on a deeper cellular level. The CO_2 then leaves our lungs.

~Exhale~

I take each breath with you in the funnel of my eyes. Fold you into the pockets that catch my tears, keep your silhouette dancing across my pupils like particles—light cut by shape, you shapeshift from you into a neon blur. Something like you when I blink to dream of the time when you actually stood before me.
No matter

~Inhale~

I trace your silhouette with the O_2 that runs its course through my pulmonary arteries. Your starry being dances a dance that sits so gentle like dew on a single blade of grass. Second breath past before I blink my eyes just to breathe you in again.

~Exhale~

Oh, be kind.
Be kind and breathe it into me.
Deep breath—breathe it into me, all that relief.
Exhale that delightful poison-laced relief of yours so I – now motionless and full might look at you; simply just look at you… and no more.
With lungs full of your relief, eyes full of your reflection. I will have the relief of taking you—taking you in on the inhale, escaping me on the exhale and that glorious empty will fill me something divine so that it will be simply a look. A look like breath, hovering between us, as you walk away.
And lips, your relief will seep, too toxic and heavy for my tongue to sleep

~Inhale~

As you exhale the toxins, I breathe you in.
Lay gently on me like the wind.
Breathe slowly across every inch of my epidermis.
~Inhale~
Lungs expand
I'll exchange my O_2 for your CO_2
~Exhale~
We reside in each other's air
Space
Cycle on repeat
Remember to keep my silhouette dancing across your pupils as you
Oxygenate me.

— Nastashia Minto & Selena Bekakis

Zrak

~Udah~

Kratak je vremenski okvir kada zrak napušta pluća. Zalazeći duboko u svaku alveolu. Povlačeći svaki element u džepove. Kolajući našim krvnim stanicama kako bi nas ispunio kisikom na dubljoj staničnoj razini. Potom CO^2 napušta naša pluća.

~Izdah~

Uvlačim svaki udah s tobom u lijevak svojih očiju. Spremam te u džepove koji love moje suze, drže tvoju siluetu koja mi pleše zjenicama poput čestica – svjetlo presječeno oblikom, pretačeš se iz sebe u neonsku mrlju. Nešto poput tebe kada trepnem kako bih sanjao o vremenu kada si ustvari stajala preda mnom.
Nije važno

~Udah~

Pratim tvoju siluetu s O^2 koja prati svoj tijek mojim plućnim arterijama. Tvoje zvjezdano biće pleše ples koji sjeda toliko nježno poput rose na vlati trave. Prođe i drugi dah prije nego trepnem
samo kako bih te opet udahnuo.

~Izdah~

Ah, budi ljubazna.
Budi ljubazna i udahni mi ga.
Dubok udah – udahni ga u mene, sve to olakšanje.
Izdahni to svoje divno otrovom okruženo olakšanje tako da te ja – sada nepomičan i pun moći gledam; samo da te gledam… i ništa više.
Pluća punih tvojeg olakšanja, očiju punih tvojeg odraza. Dobit ću olakšanje što te uzimam – uzimam te u u udahu, koji mi bježi u izdahu i ta veličanstvena praznina ispunit će me nečim toliko božanstvenim da će biti naprosto pogled.
Pogled poput daha, vrzmajući se između nas, dok odlaziš.
I usne, tvoje olakšanje će sipiti, previše otrovne i teške za moj jezik da spava

~Udah~

Dok izdišeš toksine, ja te udišem.
Nalegni blago na mene poput vjetra.
Diši polako preko svakog milimetra moje epiderma.
~Udah~
Pluća se šire
Razmijenit ću svoj O^2 za tvoj CO^2
~Izdah~
Prebivamo jedno drugome u
prostoru
krug se ponavlja
zapamti i zadrži moju siluetu koja pleše tvojim zjenicama
dok me ti
puniš kisikom.

— Nastashia Minto & Selena Bekakis
(Prijevod, Jelena Pataki)

Oras

-Įkvėpk-

Ta trumputė akimirka prieš orui išeinant iš plaučių. Jis sunkias gilyn į visus alveolių rezginius. Kilsteli kiekvieną audinio dalelę savo kely. Teka gyslomis tiekdamas deguonį mūsų ląstelėms. Tuomet CO_2 išeina iš plaučių.

-Iškvėpk-

Man kvėpuojant tavo figūra boluoja mano akių lietyje. Sulankstau tave ir įsidedu į kišenes – mano ašaros sukrenta į jas, tavo siluetas šoka mano vyzdžiuos lyg molekulės – šviesa, įdrėksta pavidalo, tu pavirsti neonine blausa. Kažkas panašus į tave sušmėžuoja, kai mirkteliu
svajingai prisimindamas, kaip tąkart stovėjai priešais mane. Nesvarbu

-Įkvėpk-

Seku tavo siluetą pasikliaudamas O_2, kuris plūsta plaučių arterijomis. Tavo žvaigždėta esybė šoka
šokį, kuris švelniai it rasa nusėda ant žolės stiebelio. Įkvepiu antrąsyk ir sumirksiu vien tam, kad šnervės ir vėl tave įtrauktų.

-Iškvėpk-

Ak, būk maloninga.
Būk gera, įsiurbk oro gūsius man į plaučius.
Kvėpuoju giliai – į mane plūsta tasai paguodos jausmas.
Iškvėpk šią džiugią, nuoduos išmirkytą savo paguodą, kad aš – sustingęs ir visagalis – galėčiau pažvelgt į tave,
tik pažvelgt... ir nieko daugiau.
Plaučiai kupini tavosios paguodos, akys sklidinos tavojo
atspindžio. Pasiguosiu tave paėmęs – tave įkvėpęs,
ištrūksi man iškvepiant ir ši didi tuštuma išsilies,
užpildys ir bus dieviška lyg paprastas žvilgsnis. Žvilgsnis, gležnas tarsi mano kvėpavimas, kurs
tvyro tarp mudviejų, tau atitolstant.
Lūpos prisirps tavosios paguodos nuodo – jis per stiprus, kad liežuvis užmigtų.

-Įkvėpk-

Tu iškvepi nuodą, aš įkvepiu nuodą.
Užgulk mane švelniai lyg vėjo gūsis.
Tegu tavo kvėpavimas iš lėto užlieja kiekvieną odos lopinėlį.
-Įkvėpk-
Plaučiai išsiplečia
Iškeisiu savo O_2 į tavo CO_2
-Iškvėpk-
Mes tūnom vienas kito ore
Erdvių
Nenutrūkstamas ciklas
Tegu mano siluetas šoka tavo vyzdžiuos, kai tu
aprūpini mane deguonim.

— Nastashia Minto & Selena Bekakis
(Vertė Dominykas Norkūnas)

Loft

~ Andaðu að þér ~

Það er lítill ramma frá því að loftið fer úr lungunum. Ná djúpt í hvert ristil. Draga upp hvern þátt í vasana. Að fara í gegnum blóðfrumur okkar til að súrefnisbæta okkur á dýpri frumu. CO2 fer síðan úr lungunum.

~ Andaðu frá þér

Ég tek hvert andardrátt með þér í trekt auganna minna. Felldu þig í vasana sem grípa tár mín, haltu skuggamyndinni þinni yfir nemendum mínum eins og agnir - létt skorið eftir lögun, þú mótar frá þér í neonþoka. Eitthvað eins og þú þegar ég blikna til að dreyma

um tímann þegar þú stóðst raunverulega fyrir mér.

Skiptir engu

~ Andaðu að þér ~

Ég rekur skuggamyndina þína með O2 sem gengur í gegnum lungnaslagæðin mín. Stjörnumerkjavera þín dansar dans sem situr svo mildur eins og dögg á einu grasblaði. Önnur andardráttur framhjá áður en ég blikna í augun bara til að anda að þér aftur.

~ Andaðu frá þér

Ó, vertu góður.
Vertu góður og andaðu því inn í mig.
Djúpt andardrátt - andaðu því inn í mig, allur sá léttir.
Andaðu frá þér þessari yndislegu eiturhúðaða léttir,

svo ég – nú hreyfingarlaus og full gæti horft á þig; einfaldlega horfa bara á þig ... og ekki meira. Með lungu fullar af léttir þínum, augu full af speglun þinni. Ég mun fá þann léttir að taka þig - taka þig með innönduninni, sleppa mér við andann og sú glæsilega tóma mun fylla mig eitthvað guðdómlegt svo það verði einfaldlega útlit. Útlit eins og andardráttur, sveima á milli okkar þegar þú gengur í burtu.
Og varir, léttir þinn mun seytla, of eitrað og þungur til að tunga mín geti sofið

~ Andaðu að þér ~

Þegar þú andar út

eiturefnunum anda ég þér inn.
Láttu varlega á mig eins og vindurinn.
Andaðu rólega yfir hvern tommu af húðþekju minni.
~ Andaðu að þér ~
Lungur stækka
Ég mun skiptast á O2 mínum fyrir CO2 þinn
~ Andaðu frá þér
Við búum í lofti hvers annars
Rými
Hringdu í endurtekningu
Mundu að halda skuggamyndinni minni dansa um nemendur þína eins og þú
Súrefni mig.

— *Nastashia Minto & Selena Bekakis*
(Þýtt úr Ensku, Michael Lohr)

Aire

~Inhalar ~

Hay un pequeño intervalo de tiempo desde el momento en que el aire sale de los pulmones. Cuando está penetrando profundamente en cada cama de alvéolos. Levantando cada elemento en los bolsillos. Atravesando nuestras células sanguíneas para oxigenarnos a un nivel celular más profundo. El CO_2 entonces sale de nuestros pulmones.

~Exhalar~

Tomo cada respiración contigo en el embudo de mis ojos. Te doblo en los bolsillos que atrapan mis lágrimas, mantengo tu silueta que baila entre mis alumnos como partículas — luz cortada por la forma, cambias de forma de ti a un aspecto borrón de neón. Algo como tú cuando parpadeo para soñar con el tiempo cuando en realidad estabas delante de mí. No importa

Rastreo tu silueta con el O_2 que recorre a través de mis arterias pulmonares. Tu ser estrellado baila un baile que se sienta tan dulce como el rocío en una sola hoja de hierba. El segundo aliento pasó antes de que parpadeo mis ojos sólo para respirarte de nuevo.

~Exhalar~

Ah, se amable.
Se amable y respira en mí.
Respira profundamente, respira en mí, todo ese alivio.
Exhala ese delicioso alivio envenenado tuyo para que yo — ahora inmóvil y llena podría mirarte; simplemente mirarte... y no más.
Con pulmones llenos de su alivio, ojos llenos de su reflexión. Tendré el alivio de inhalarte — recogiéndote a la inhalación, de que me escapas en la exhalación, y ese vacío glorioso me llenará de algo divino para que sea simplemente una mirada. Una mirada como el aliento, flotando entre nosotros, mientras te alejas.
Y los labios, tu alivio se filtrará, demasiado tóxico y pesado para que mi lengua duerma

~Inhalar~
Como tu exhalas las toxinas, te respiro.
Suavemente acuéstate sobre mí como el viento.
Respira lentamente en cada pulgada de mi epidermis.
~inhalar~
Los pulmones se amplían
Cambiaré mi O_2 por su CO_2
~exhalar~
Residemos en el aire de cada uno
Espacio
Ciclo del otro en repetir
Recuerda mantener mi silueta bailando a través de tus pupilas mientras
me oxigenas.

— *Nastashia Minto y Selena Bekakis*
(traducción, T. Warburton y Bajo y rvb)

//
michael fikaris
//
end points / puntos finales /
krajnja tocke / lokapunktar
//
made for **hold on** exhib.,
rubicon art,
melbourne,
vic.,
oz.,
7—24 nov., 2018
//

//
michael fikaris
//
end points / puntos finales /
krajnja tocke / lokaatriđi
//
made for **hold on** exhib.,
rubicon art,
melbourne,
vic.,
oz.,
7—24 nov., 2018
//

Kurt Eisenlohr
three works (portfolio)

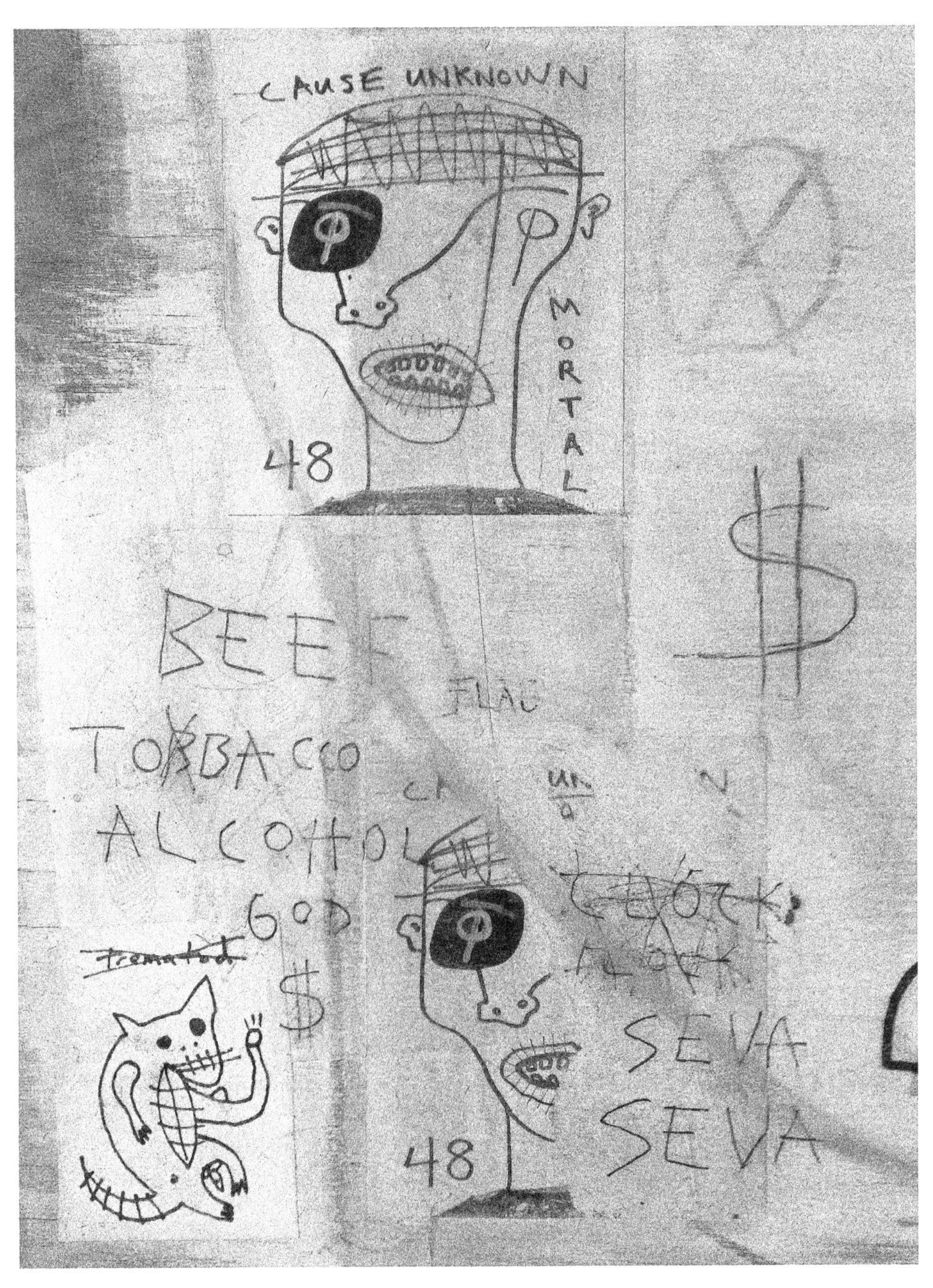
CAUSE UNKNOWN
MORTAL
48
BEEF
ALCOHOL
GOD
$
SEVA
SEVA
48

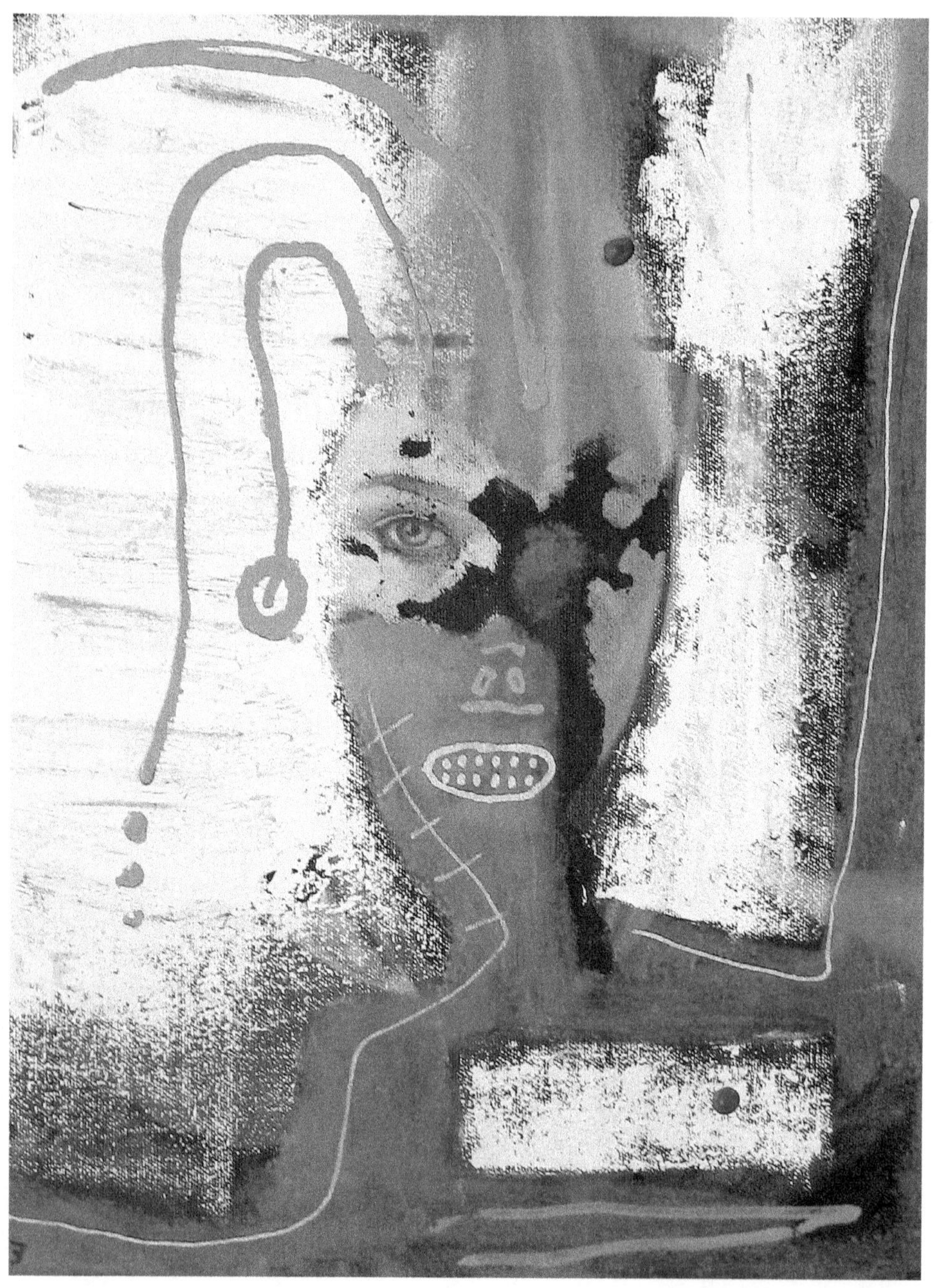

Nisva

Andrej Blatnik

Kadar sem sploh lahko zaspala, je bilo v redu. A kadar nisem mogla spati, sem mislila nate in na najino prihodnost. Vedela sem, da bo kratka. Seveda bova kmalu spala skupaj. A kaj se bo potem spremenilo? Nisva, ki bi lahko bila skupaj, saj to veva oba, skupaj in vsak zase. In vendar sem šla s tabo na vse te kave, ki že dolgo niso bile več samo kave, in vse te kozarčke, kdo bi se spomnil, kaj je bilo v njih. In sva vsakič vedela, da nisva. In vendar si me vabil zmeraj znova in jaz sem zmeraj znova rekla, da mogoče, da lahko, da dajva, nikoli nisem rekla, da nisva. Morda bi morala reči takoj, ko sem vedela, a vedela sem takoj, in potem ne bi bilo nobenih kav, nobenih kozarčkov, nobenih vabil. Potem bi morala reči sama sebi: nisem. To zveni tako samotno. Nisva, to je bolje, dosti bolje. *Q*

We're Not

Andrej Blatnik

(Tr. fr. the Slovenian, Tamara M. Soban)

It was okay when I managed to sleep. But when I couldn't, I'd think about you and our future. I knew it wouldn't last. Sure, we'd soon sleep together. But what would that change? We're not a good match, we both know that, together and apart. And yet I went for all those coffees with you, coffees that had long ceased being just coffees, and all those drinks, who could remember what they were. And we knew every time that we're not. And yet you asked me out over and over again, and over and over again I said maybe, okay, let's, I never said that we're not. Maybe I should've said it the moment I knew it; but I knew it straight away and then there would've been no coffees, no drinks, no invitations. Then I should've told myself: I'm not. That sounds so lonesome. We're not is better, much better. *Q*

Nismo

Andrej Blatnik

(Prijevod, Jagna Pogačnik)

Kad bih uopće mogla zaspati, bilo bi u redu. Ali kad nisam mogla spavati, mislila sam na tebe i našu budućnost. Znala sam da će biti kratka. Naravno da ćemo uskoro skupa spavati. Ali što će se potom promijeniti? Nismo oni koji bi mogli biti zajedno, oboje to znamo, skupa i svatko za sebe. A ipak sam išla s tobom na sve te kave koje već dugo nisu bile samo kave, i sve te čašice, tko bi se sjećao što je u njima bilo. I svaki smo put znali da nismo. A ipak si me zvao uvijek ponovo i ja sam uvijek ponovo rekla da možda, da može, da haj'mo, nikad nisam rekla da nismo. Možda sam morala reći odmah kad sam znala, a znala sam odmah, i onda ne bi bilo nikakvih kava, nikakvih čašica, nikakvih poziva. Onda bih morala reći sama sebi: nisam. To zvuči tako samotno. Nismo, to je bolje, puno bolje. *Q*

Nismo

Andrej Blatnik

(Prevod, Ivan Antić)

Tek kad sam mogla da zaspim, bilo je bolje. Dok mi san nije hteo na oči, mislila sam na tebe i našu budućnost. Znala sam da kratka će biti. Naravno da ćemo uskoro voditi ljubav. I šta će onda biti drukčije? Nismo mi od onih što mogu, znamo oboje to, i zajedno i svako za sebe. A ipak odlazila sam s tobom na sve te kafe, koje već dugo nisu bile samo kafe, i sva ta pića, i ko bi se uopšte mogao setiti šta je sve bilo u tim čašama. I svaki put, znali smo da nismo. Međutim, ti si me uvek iznova zvao i ja sam uvek iznova rekla *da, možda* ili *da, može* ili *da, idemo*, a nikad nisam rekla da nismo. Trebalo je da kažem čim sam znala da je tako, a znala sam odmah, pa onda ne bi bilo ni kafa, ni pića, ni bilo kakvih poziva. Ali onda bih morala samoj sebi reći: nisam. A to zvuči tako usamljenički. Nismo, to zvuči bolje, mnogo bolje. *Q*

Не сме

АНДРЕЈ БЛАТНИК
(Превод, Пидија Димковска)

Добро беше кога воопшто можев да заспијам. А кога не можев да спијам мислев на тебе и на нашата иднина. Знаев дека ќе биде куса. Секако дека наскоро ќе спиеме заедно. Но што ќе смени тоа? Не сме ние тие кои би требало да бидат заедно, па тоа го знаеме и двајцата заедно и секој посебно. А сепак, одев со тебе на сите оние кафиња кои веќе долго не беа само кафиња, и на сите оние чашки пијалак, ама кој да се сети што имаше во нив. И секојпат знаевме дека не сме. А сепак ме канеше секогаш одново и јас секогаш одново велев дека ќе видам, дека може, па ајде, а никогаш не реков дека не сме. Требаше веднаш да кажам кога веќе знаев, а знаев веднаш, и потоа немаше да има никакви кафиња, никакви чашки пијалак, никакви покани. Потоа ќе требаше сама да си речам себеси: не сум. Но тоа звучи толку самотно. Не сме, тоа е подобро, многу подобро.Q

No somos

Andrej Blatnik
(Traducción, Marjeta Drobnič)

Cuando lograba dormirme al menos un rato, todo estaba bien. Pero cuando no podía dormir, pensaba en ti y en nuestro futuro. Sabía que sería corto. No tardaremos en acostarnos, claro. ¿Pero qué cambiará después? No somos de los que se quedan juntos, lo sabemos los dos, juntos y por separado. Y, sin embargo, he ido contigo a tomarme todos esos cafés, que llevan tiempo no siendo sólo cafés, y todas esas copas, quién recordaría qué contenían. Y cada vez sabíamos que no éramos. Y, sin embargo, me invitabas una y otra vez y yo te decía una y otra vez que a lo mejor, que podíamos, que venga, nunca he dicho que no somos. Tal vez debiera decirlo en cuanto lo supe, pero lo supe enseguida, y, luego, no habría habido cafés ni nada, ni copas, ni invitaciones. Y debería decirme a mí misma: no soy. Lo cual suena tan solitario. No somos, así es mejor, mucho mejor. Q

MICHAEL FIKARIS

PEREGRINO INÚTIL

(traducción, T. Warburton y Bajo y rvb)

futile pèlerin

(traduction, jérôme bihan)

PEREGRINO INÚTIL

(tradução, marcos farrajota)

nenaudingas piligrimas

(Iš anglų kalbos vertė, miglė anušauskaitė)

HACK

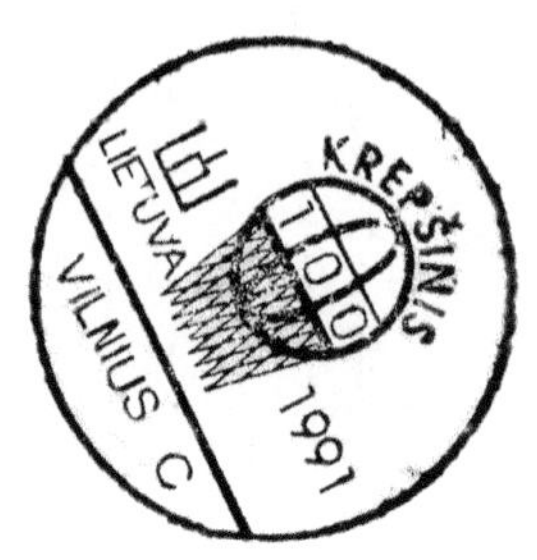

MACHETAZO

abattre

abater

čiaukšt

HACK

MACHETAZO

abattre

abater

čiaukšt

CULTURE IS NEEDED HERE

LA CULTURA ES NECESARIA AQUÍ

ce lieu a besoin de culture

é necessária cultura aqui

čia reikėtų kultūros

Y AQUÍ, ASÍ COMO ESTÁ ALLÍ... ¡NADA!

et ici, à cet endroit précis...rein!

e aqui, tal e qual como ali... —nada!

o čia, kaip ir ten... - nieko!

AND I AM THE ONE TO BRING IT TO THIS PREHISTORIC OF PLACES!

STARTING HERE...
...JUST LIKE THIS

¡Y YO SOY EL QUE LA TRAE A ESTE LUGAR PREHIS-
TÓRICO

et je suis celui qui l'introduira dans ce lieu reculé

e eu serei quem trazê-la para este ermo pré-históri-
co!

ir būtent aš ją atnešiu į šią priešistorinę vietą!

COMIENZO AQUÍ...
...ASÍ COMO ESTO...

et commençant par ici...
...et comme ceci

cemeçando aquí...
...assím mesmo

pradėsiu nuo čia...
...štai taip